A Wicked
for the Marque

THE FAIRBOURNE SISTERS

BOOK 2

A Steamy Historical Regency Romance Novel

by

Valentina Lovelace

RUBEDIA
PUBLISHING

Disclaimer & Copyright

This is a work of fiction. Names, characters, places, and incidents are either products of the author's imagination or are used fictitiously. Any resemblance to actual events, locales, or persons, living or dead, is entirely coincidental.

Table of Contents

Letter from Valentina Lovelace

Hello, darling!

I'm Valentina Lovelace, a hopeless romantic with a wicked imagination and a love for all things Regency. If there's a secret rendezvous, a scandal brewing, or a duke about to be undone, I'm there, probably taking notes.

I write steamy love stories where danger lurks behind every fan flutter and heroines never wait politely for permission. My stories are for readers who like their romance with sharp tongues, slow teases, and absolutely no chill.

Off the page, I'm raising two tiny, adorable, future scandal-makers, believing I'm in control of the household (I'm not), pretending tea is a personality trait, and occasionally convincing my husband to "act out" plot research.

If you're into bold women, bad decisions, and ballroom gossip turned foreplay — welcome. I've been expecting you!

Till our next whispered word,

Valentina Lovelace

Chapter One

"He is gone," her father said flatly without so much as a glance in her direction.

Catharine Fairbourne did not immediately respond. She sat perfectly still on the damask settee with her back so rigid her spine might have been forged of iron, though her hands, which were hidden in the folds of her dove-grey muslin, were clenched tightly in her lap.

"He left in the night," Mr. Fairbourne continued, pacing before the marble hearth. "With the merchant's daughter... of all things."

The word *merchant* seemed to linger on his tongue like something bitter. The fire crackled as if in mockery, casting flickers of orange across his sharply tailored coat, the high black collar shadowing his weathered face.

Catharine blinked slowly. Her breath had stilled in her throat, like frost settling on a windowpane. It wasn't heartbreak this time, not quite. That had happened once before, and it had not come back the same way. What she felt now was something much more ancient.

It was a slow, spreading shame.

The pale silk wallpaper behind her seemed to close in as the silver patterns twisted and writhed less like vines and more like chains. The air smelled faintly of beeswax polish and crushed lavender. That had always been her mother's choice, meant to soothe, but it did not soothe. Not today.

"He left you, Catharine." Her father turned to face her now. "With no explanation but passion and impudence. Do you comprehend what this means? Three days before the wedding. The invitations are sent. The carriages ordered."

She swallowed. The taste in her mouth was iron. "Yes," she said softly. "I comprehend it."

Mr. Fairbourne's nostrils flared. "It's the second time. *The second.* You must see how this reflects on you."

She did not flinch, though a thin crack fissured through her composure. Just behind her ribs, something trembled, like porcelain struck by a sudden draft.

Her gaze dropped to the carpet. She tried to focus her sight on a pattern of woven roses, dusty with age and footfall. The first time had been Edmund Weatherby. She had been one and twenty. She was young and far too trusting, though everyone had said she was the clever one. And still he had left for a baronet's daughter with dimples and no opinions.

And now the viscount. He'd left her for a woman who sold lace.

"Have you nothing to say?" her father asked.

Her fingers tightened around the folds of her dress until her knuckles whitened. "What should I say?"

"That you regret allowing this... this *embarrassment* to befall you. That you are *ashamed.* That you understand the difficulty this puts upon the family." He spoke as if reading from one of his ledgers: no emotion, mere factual reason.

Shame. There it was, that word again. It hung in the room like a damp fog, clinging to the curtains, the walls, the very fabric of her skin, tainting her.

Catharine lifted her chin slowly. Her pale eyes, cool as moonlight, met her father's. "I *am* ashamed."

The words cost her more than she thought they would. Her throat felt raw around them.

Mr. Fairbourne gave a single nod, as if he had merely been waiting to hear the proper litany. Then he turned back to the fire, his hands still locked behind his back, as if signifying his impotence in the only affair that truly mattered to him.

"You will remain indoors until I decide what is to be done. No visitors. And for God's sake, stay away from the windows."

She stood up. "Of course." Her voice was glass: thin, hard, and liable to shatter.

She walked from the drawing room with slow precision, her steps soundless against the thick carpet. The house was hushed, suffocating in its civility. Upstairs, in her rooms, she closed the door hastily and leaned back against it, almost as if in an effort to prevent shame from entering. But it followed her, nonetheless. It always would.

Her reflection in the mirror did not tremble. But she did. She had been left again. Fortunately, there was no love. It was mere pragmatism of the fact that, as the eldest daughter of three and twenty, she should marry and bring prosperity to her family. There was no romantic tragedy, only mortification, only failure, only the quiet certainty that whatever was wrong with her was not something she could name or fix.

That was when she broke. A single, fragile exhale trembled loose from her chest, like a bird caged for far too long. She moved towards the window with the slow deliberation of a sleepwalker, and when she could no longer bear the weight inside her, she sank to her knees before the chaise and pressed her forehead to the cushion.

The tears came then, sudden and ungraceful, scalding her cheeks with their heat. This was no silent, noble weeping. No. This was a helpless leaking of everything she had held in through her father's words, through the firelight, through the empty click of the drawing-room clock that had sounded like the end of something.

A sob stabbed her with the fire of a knife, shameful in its honesty. And then she heard a knock.

The door creaked open before she could speak, and Margaret's light, unmistakable tread crossed the room. "Catharine?"

Catharine scrambled up, too quickly. She wiped her cheeks with her sleeve, the wetness stubborn and clinging. "You shouldn't be here."

Margaret stopped only a few paces in. Her cheeks were flushed, her golden hair slightly windblown as if she'd been running up the stairs that, only a moment ago, had separated the two sisters.

"I... I heard Papa."

Catharine turned her back, overwhelmed by shame. "Then you know."

There was a pause. Then the rustle of skirts as Margaret approached. "May I sit?"

Catharine gave no answer, but Margaret did anyway, settling beside her on the chaise, careful not to crowd her. They sat in silence for what felt like an eternity. Catharine stared at her reflection in the dark window. Her face was blotched. Her nose slightly red. She looked like someone else... someone weak.

"I'm sorry," Margaret said softly.

Catharine didn't reply. Her throat was too tight. But Margaret waited, like she always did when she meant to be kind, with her hands folded neatly in her lap and her eyes wide and earnest.

It undid her.

With a breath that wavered and cracked, Catharine leaned forward, resting her elbows on her knees. Then she let her face fall into her hands.

"I can't do it again, Margaret." Her voice was low, hollowed out of a million anguishes. "I can't attend another ball alone. I can't smile at people who pity me. I can't hear them whispering *She is the one who was left, again.*"

Margaret's hand touched hers, featherlight.

"No one ever chooses me. They look, and they consider, but they don't choose. Not really. Not when it matters." Catharine swallowed back another sob. "And now they won't even pretend to. I'm becoming a warning. A… spinster."

Margaret's voice was gentle but sure. "You're not a warning. You're not done."

"I *am.*" Catharine's voice sharpened, brittle with despair. "Who would want me now? I have two engagements behind me, both having ended in scandal. I'm not silly or charming or…" She paused, spitting out the rest, *"like you."*

The words landed heavily. Catharine regretted them instantly. But Margaret didn't flinch. Instead, she moved closer, wrapping her arm lightly around her sister's shoulders. Catharine allowed it. Just this once.

"Catharine," Margaret whispered, "you don't have to face them tomorrow. Or next week. Or this year, if you don't want to."

Catharine gave a hollow laugh, wet with irony. "We don't get to vanish, Margaret. Not women like us. We smile, and we go to teas, and we answer politely when someone asks what became of our future. And then we pretend we've never known longing."

Margaret squeezed her arm. "Then don't pretend. Not with me."

Catharine sat back from Margaret at last, brushing the dampness from her cheeks with the heel of her hand. Her voice, when it came again, was quieter now.

"I've ruined everything."

Margaret frowned. "Don't say that."

"It's true." Catharine folded her hands in her lap, her fingers knotting together with unconscious tension. "Do you think I don't know what they're saying already? I was *jilted*, Margaret. *Twice.* What suitor in his right mind would court into this family now, when the oldest daughter has turned scandal into a pattern?"

"You didn't turn anything—"

"It doesn't matter what's true." Catharine's eyes flicked towards the dark windowpane again. "It only matters what's believable. And right now, I am a burden to our name."

Margaret reached for her again, but Catharine stood abruptly, pacing to the edge of the hearth.

"You should distance yourself from me," she said, her back to her sister. "Fortunately, Eliza is already married. But you... you're still young, still full of hope. But if they start whispering that it runs in the family, that *Fairbourne women* drive men away... what then? You'll have your pick reduced to fortune-hunters and third sons with debts and nothing else."

Margaret rose too, her voice tight with disbelief. "You cannot mean that."

Catharine turned slowly. "I do." She meant every word of it, even if it hurt to say it. *Especially* because it hurt. "I have no illusions left. None. But you... you still can have all the things I won't. I'll not spoil your chances by hovering behind you at garden parties with a smile too tight and a name too tarnished."

Margaret stepped forward. "You're not ruined, Catharine. You've just been unlucky. Society's judgement doesn't last forever, not if—"

"It does if you give them nothing else to talk about." Catharine exhaled and let the words rise from the dark place in her chest where she'd buried them.

"Then... what?" Margaret's voice cracked, as if herself afraid of the answer she had asked for.

Then what indeed? The answer was clear as daylight. A woman either married or remained a spinster and brought shame upon her family. In all honesty, there was nothing to think about, nothing to consider or reconsider.

"I will *marry*, Margaret. I don't care if the groom is a widower or a tradesman's son or someone with a title he won playing cards. I will not be paraded again as the girl who almost became a viscountess but couldn't hold him."

Margaret's mouth parted in a silent protest. Then she hesitated but still decided to speak. "If you truly mean that, there is someone who might... help."

Catharine blinked. "Help?"

Margaret looked down, then back up, her expression torn between mischief and fear. "It's only a whisper, really. Something Lady Merton mentioned once at luncheon. About Lady Leclair."

The name landed like a thunderclap in the room.

Catharine narrowed her eyes. "That... charlatan?"

"She uhm... *arranges* things," Margaret said cautiously. "Discreetly. Especially for women in... well, in positions like yours. Or worse. It's all rather clandestine and dreadfully unspoken, but she finds matches. Real ones. And quickly."

Catharine didn't move for a long moment. "I've heard she deals in transactions, not romance."

"Well, who needs romance," Margaret said, almost defiantly, "when one needs results?"

That gave Catharine pause. A strange, sharp calm began to unfurl inside her, like a new bodice laced too tightly around an unfamiliar shape. She didn't want affection. She didn't need sentiment. She needed salvation that was fast, clean, and most importantly, complete.

"How would I reach her?" she asked, her voice like a struck match.

Margaret lifted an eyebrow. "You're serious?"

"I have three days," Catharine said. Her chin lifted. "That's enough time for desperation. And miracles. And not a moment more."

Margaret hesitated. "She only sees women in the mornings. You'd have to leave before breakfast. I think she's in Brackley Square."

Catharine turned away and looked towards her armoire, already calculating what she would wear. It would have to be something plain, something that would allow her to conceal her identity, something dignified but not cold. The resolve settled in her chest like steel.

Then she looked back over her shoulder.

"Thank you," she said and meant it.

Margaret came to her side again and touched her hand. "Just promise me one thing."

"What is it?"

"That you won't marry someone cruel. Even if they'll have you."

Catharine felt as if someone reached into her chest and grabbed her by the heart, squeezing tightly. "There's no cruelty worse than what society is already doing to me."

And yet, deep in the silent chambers of her heart, where pride had not yet killed every dream, she wondered if that were truly so.

Chapter Two

Catharine had never entered a home like this before. Not even in the grandest corners of Mayfair had she seen opulence this garish, this determinedly ostentatious. The entry hall alone glittered with gold-trimmed mirrors and sconces shaped like serpentine vines. Overhead, a chandelier of coloured glass dripped like fruit from the ceiling, casting jewel-toned shadows across the floor.

She swallowed hard, feeling her heart tapping quickly against her ribs.

The butler, a tall, impassive man with white gloves and a stare that looked right through her, was brief but not impolite.

"This way, Lady Davis." He ushered her down the hallway.

Lady Davis.

The name still sat awkwardly on her tongue, for it was a makeshift disguise sewn from desperation. She had borrowed the title from an imaginary husband, a fictional country squire whose last breath had conveniently spared her the indignity of spinsterhood. The maid's clothing, however, was not fiction. The gown she wore was one of Rose's old uniforms: plain brown wool, a bit too tight at the waist and short at the wrists. She'd kept her hair tucked beneath a modest cap, her only vanity a single pin to hold it in place.

Every step forward made her more aware of the lie she was carrying. And yet she held her chin steady and reminded herself that there was no other choice.

Then they reached the parlour, and the door opened with a dramatic sweep.

Lady Leclair was already there, waiting. She did not rise to greet her.

She reclined on a velvet settee, one slippered foot tucked beneath her, the other dangling carelessly over the side. She was draped in layers of plum silk and midnight gauze with bangles stacked along her arms and rings glittering from nearly every finger. To Catharine, they appeared more like treasure than jewellery.

Her skin was warm-toned, smooth and theatrical, as though she'd been painted in oils and left half-finished. Her dark hair was wrapped in a towering silk turban, pinned with a glinting crescent moon that caught the light like a secret.

Her eyes were almond-shaped and lined with kohl, flicking up to Catharine with interest, not warmth.

"Lady Davis?" Lady Leclair purred at last, her accent fluid and unplaceable. She tilted her head slightly, her eyes roaming over Catharine's plain gown. "I assumed you would come dressed discreetly. But I must say, this is a marvel of understatement. You could almost pass for someone unimportant."

Catharine flushed beneath the barb, though she suspected it had been half a compliment. "I wished to be... unremarkable."

"Oh, darling," Lady Leclair drawled, waving a perfumed hand through the air. "No one comes to me to remain unremarkable. Sit."

The parlour was saturated in colour and scent with incense curling sweetly from a brass burner on the mantel, surrounded by upholstery in a riot of peacock tones. Heavy velvet curtains dimmed the morning light to a kind of eternal twilight. It felt more like stepping into a stage set than a sitting room.

Catharine perched on the edge of the chair across from the matchmaker, her back perfectly straight despite the uneven stuffing beneath her.

Lady Leclair watched her for a long, silent moment. "So... another woman wronged." Her tone was dry but not unkind.

Catharine kept her voice even. "I was to be married, but the groom fled with... someone else."

A gleam of unexpected interest passed through Lady Leclair's gaze. "And you still wish to marry?"

"I *must*," Catharine said quickly, surprising herself with the urgency in her voice. "I will not endure another season as a subject of pity. I will not live in my sister's shadow. I must marry, and I do not care for romance or rank."

Lady Leclair leaned back, one ringed hand lifting to tap her chin. "So practical. And yet so... tight." Her fingers made a vague gesture, as if Catharine were something bound up tightly in ribbon. "It's always the ones like you who are most difficult to place. Not because you are unworthy. But because you carry a storm inside you. And most men prefer their wives silent as a portrait."

Catharine stared back, unsure whether to bristle or accept the observation.

Lady Leclair sighed, the sound almost theatrical. "Very well. Let us see what we can salvage from the scandal. But I warn you, Lady Davis, I deal in matches of necessity, not fantasy. I find husbands. Not saviours. And the men who come to me... they often have their own reputations to mend."

"I don't care," Catharine said, her voice cold as marble. "So long as the wedding happens."

17

Lady Leclair grinned, allowing her white teeth to flash behind her painted lips. "Then let us begin."

And with a flick of her hand, she reached for a ledger bound in red leather. To Catharine, it seemed thicker than a Bible and infinitely more damning. The woman opened the crimson ledger with a flick so practiced that it was almost theatrical. The pages whispered as she turned them, a chorus of doomed romances and desperate arrangements.

"Now," she said, scanning her entries, "tell me again, how soon do you need this miraculous union to occur?"

Catharine lifted her chin. "Three days."

There was a pause.

Lady Leclair slowly lowered the book to her lap, blinked once, then let out a bark of laughter. "*Three* days? My dear, this is a matchmaking salon, not the Second Coming."

"I am quite serious," Catharine said, as levelly as if she were ordering tea. "The guests are already invited. The banns were posted. The flowers have been delivered. If I don't replace him, there will be whispers for decades, and not the sort one survives with her dignity intact."

Lady Leclair stared at her, one brow arching so high it nearly touched the jewelled moon on her turban. "Do you wish for a wedding or a hostage negotiation?"

Catharine stood, straightening her modest skirts. "Fine. If you cannot help me, I shall take my leave."

Lady Leclair opened her mouth, perhaps to make another quip, but Catharine had already turned. Her heart thudded heavily, each step towards the door louder than the last.

It had been foolish to come here. Foolish to hope.

"Wait."

The word snapped through the air like the crack of a whip. Catharine paused, with her hand already on the doorknob.

Lady Leclair sighed, and when she spoke again, her tone had changed. There were fewer sparkles and a lot more steel.

"There is... one possibility," she said slowly, as if regretting it already. "But I hesitate to suggest it."

Catharine turned back. "Why?"

Lady Leclair tapped her lacquered fingernails against the arm of the settee, rhythmic and thoughtful. "Because he is not a man most women wish to marry. Not unless they are... very determined, or very desperate."

"Both apply," Catharine said dryly. "Who is he?"

There was hesitation, a silence that was filled with something akin to dread. Then words that shattered the silence.

"Lord Alaric Vale. The Marquess of Ravensedge."

The name dropped like a stone into the silence.

Catharine's breath caught, her spine tightening instinctively. "The beast of Hampshire?"

Lady Leclair gave a languid shrug. "I suppose that's one of the kinder nicknames. But yes. One and the same."

Catharine's mind immediately conjured the gossip, the shadows, and scraps of scandal passed in drawing rooms like parlour games. He was a man with a vicious scar down his cheek, given to storming out of salons mid-conversation. He had a wild temper and unmatched crippling cynicism. He had been a recluse in the country for years until he'd recently reemerged, brooding and bristling, in an effort to mend his reputation just enough to sit in the House of Lords. Needless to say, it hadn't happened yet.

"No one's ever seen him smile," Catharine murmured aloud.

"And with good reason," Lady Leclair replied. "The poor man's life reads like a gothic novel. Family tragedy, war injury..." She waved a hand. "You know how it goes. But. He *is* looking for a wife. For reasons that are no more romantic than your own. And he moves quickly, when he bothers to move at all."

Catharine hesitated, the weight of the name Ravensedge thick in her mouth. "Would he marry a woman jilted by another man?"

Lady Leclair laughed softly. "My dear, he'd marry a foxhound if it cleared the path to the Lords. You, at least, have excellent posture."

It was a jest. But not quite.

Catharine swallowed. Her hands were cold at her sides. "Would he agree to a wedding in three days?"

Lady Leclair tilted her head, eyes narrowing in calculation. "He might. But he'll probably want something in return. Legitimacy, respectability. Obedience."

"I'm not very good at obedience," Catharine muttered.

"Excellent," Lady Leclair said with an amused grin. "Perhaps you'll bring out the worst in each other and find it... oddly companionable."

There was a pause. Catharine looked down at her plain skirts, at the faint smudge of ash on her sleeve from the hearth at home. This wasn't a fairy tale. It never had been. But it could still be a way forward, so she simply lifted her chin.

"Send word to him. Tell him Lady Davis is available. And ready to marry."

Lady Leclair's grin widened, sharp and strange.

"Oh, darling," she said, reaching once more for her ledger, "this is going to be deliciously disastrous."

"Why?" Catharine inquired curiously. "You cannot possibly mean to tell me that I am the worst case you've ever had."

Lady Leclair laughed. It was an elegant trill, almost musical, but with something sly coiled beneath it.

"Oh no, darling. Not the worst. There was once a widow who tried to trade me her cousin in exchange for a viscount with gout. And another who showed up drunk with a parrot on her shoulder."

Catharine blinked. "You're joking."

"I never joke about parrots," Lady Leclair said solemnly. Then she leaned forward, folding her hands beneath her chin, the bangles chiming like tiny bells. "But you... you are one of the most desperate I've seen. And desperation," she added with a knowing look, "makes people either terribly dull or very interesting."

Catharine exhaled sharply through her nose. "I should thank you, I suppose, for such a rousing endorsement."

"Take it as a compliment, *Lady Davis*," Lady Leclair said, lounging back again. "You're not simpering. You're not lying to yourself about what you want. That alone sets you apart. But..."—she raised one long finger—"there's a complication."

Catharine stiffened. "Of course there is."

Lady Leclair smiled. "You'll have to approach Lord Ravensedge yourself."

The room seemed to still.

Catharine stared at her incredulously. "You're not going to make the introduction?"

Lady Leclair waved her jewelled fingers delicately, as if batting the very idea away. "I've worked with rogues, rakes, and the occasionally reformed highwayman, but *he*?" She gave a shiver for dramatic effect. "He's volatile. And prickly. The last woman I sent his way left in tears and threatened to sue me for emotional assault."

"That was... an option?"

"Only in Scotland," she murmured, then fixed Catharine with a look. "Listen to me, Lady Davis... He's not the sort who responds well to mediators. He hates games. He hates matchmaking. He despises *me,* though I suspect that's because I told him his cravat looked like a dead squirrel once."

Catharine swallowed hard. "And you expect me to go to him? Uninvited?"

"You're not uninvited. You're... unannounced. There's a difference," Lady Leclair said with a wink. "Go to his house. Be honest. Lay out your proposal plainly. Don't fawn. Don't flatter. He's like an injured wolf: he'll snarl, but he's more afraid of you than you are of him."

"I sincerely doubt that," Catharine muttered.

Lady Leclair shrugged. "You'll see."

The silence stretched between them, broken only by the soft hiss of the incense curling towards the ceiling. Somewhere outside, a carriage rumbled by. Catharine's thoughts tangled and frayed at the edges. She could feel panic, disbelief, and strangely enough, an absurd flutter of excitement.

Could she really do this? March up to a man like *that* and suggest they marry before the end of the week?

No. Absolutely not. But what was the alternative?

She thought of her father's bitter scowl, of the way he'd looked at her, like she were something cracked and shameful. She thought of Margaret, still untainted, still full of sweetness and chances. And she thought of the next ball, the next season, the next unbearable year of waiting by the wall.

This was the only door left open. And though it looked like it might lead to the mouth of a dragon, it was still a door.

Catharine rose slowly from her chair. Her knees felt oddly light, but her spine straightened.

"I suppose," she said quietly, "that if I want to rescue myself, I'll have to do it alone."

Lady Leclair grinned, evidently pleased.

Catharine hesitated at the threshold, then turned back. "Does he really have a scar?"

"Oh, yes," Lady Leclair said. "And a voice like thunder. But his eyes,"—she tilted her head as she spoke—"those are the real danger."

Catharine nodded once and left the room, her heart thudding harder with every step. The air outside had cooled by the time Catharine descended the front steps of Lady Leclair's townhouse.

"Farewell, Miss *Fairbourne*," Lady Leclair called sweetly from the parlour just as the butler was opening the door.

Catharine paused, but only for a heartbeat. She didn't look back. Neither of them acknowledged the slip, or the truth of it.

The streets of London blurred around her, a watercolour of soot-stained façades and the faint perfume of noon. By the time she reached the edge of town where hired coaches waited, her false name clung to her like a too-thin cloak.

Lady Davis. Widow. Nobody.

She whispered it again inside the carriage, trying to make it feel real. It didn't. But it would have to be enough.

The journey to Hampshire was long and unwelcoming. Rain began somewhere near Reading and followed her the rest of the way like a persistent shadow, lashing at the windows and drumming on the roof in wild rhythms. The coach groaned over rutted roads, the wheels thick with mud. And still, she didn't turn back.

Ravensedge Hall loomed before her like a cliff of blackened marble, stark against the mist. Its many gables jutted like spines, its towering windows all dark save for one flickering with uncertain light. Ivy curled along the stone like veins, and somewhere faint and very far off, a raven called once, then fell silent.

Catharine stared up at it, drenched by atmosphere, chilled to the bone.

So this was the place she was willing to gamble her future on. She could feel it, something ancient and wary in the air. As though the house itself watched her from behind those blank windows, judging her as a trespasser. Or worse... an offering.

It would be so easy to turn away. To step back into the carriage and let it carry her to anywhere but *here*.

But she didn't. Instead, she stepped forward. Then, before fear could trick her into stillness, she reached out and knocked.

Once... twice... three times.

The door stood silent, and Catharine wondered if she had just knocked on the gates of her own undoing.

Chapter Three

The door closed behind her with a soft click, the sound unnervingly final. Catharine was now standing still with her spine taut as the servant retreated, leaving her alone in the study's hushed gloom.

Behind the writing table sat Lord Alaric Vale, the Marquess of Ravensedge. He did not rise to greet her.

"Finally," he said, voice low and rough, as if it had been scraped against stone. "I was expecting you earlier."

His silver-grey eyes met hers, and something inside her went utterly still. They were bright, like cold steel catching sunlight. Her heart beat once, hard. Her brow furrowed, though she kept her face carefully neutral. She had not intended to look at him, and yet she could not force herself to look away.

Expecting her?

She had not written to request this audience. There had been no time for that. But she swallowed the question, as she always did when instinct warned her not to speak. He was a man who invited silence. The weight of his presence filled the room like a storm that hadn't broken yet.

"Come here."

The command was quiet, but it vibrated through her, low and sure as thunder. She told herself she didn't hesitate, though her legs took a heartbeat too long to move. She stepped forward with her pace deliberate. When she reached the edge of the writing table, he stood.

He was taller than she'd imagined. Broad across the shoulders, solid with the kind of strength forged rather than inherited. His dark hair brushed his collar, for it was too long for fashion and too unconcerned for society. But it was not the height nor the power of him that stole her breath. It was his face.

The left side bore a jagged scar that ran from temple to jaw, a brutal relic that hadn't healed cleanly. It should have repulsed her. Yet it didn't. It... fascinated her.

The other side of his face was untouched. It was striking in its symmetry and also sharp in its beauty, but it was the contrast that made him impossible to look away from. One half a general's command, the other a poet's ruin.

Catharine had seen men try to hide their flaws. He made no attempt. The scar was not a shame to him. It was part of the battlefield he carried into every room.

And God help her, she felt herself *drawn* to him.

Her pulse betrayed her, quickening in her throat. She folded her hands before her to still them.

Control yourself.

He let the silence stretch until it frayed at the edges, until her carefully stitched composure felt in danger of unravelling. His gaze swept over her then, slow and unmistakably deliberate, from the high collar of her travelling coat to the modest hem of her gown. He studied her not as a gentleman might examine a lady but as a tactician might consider a new weapon: dangerous, perhaps, but untested.

"You are not the usual type Lady Miriam sends," he mused at last, almost as if talking to himself. "But... you'll do."

Her brows drew together. *I'll do?* A frown threatened to appear on her otherwise calm mask of a face.

"You may remove your coat."

Her breath caught. "My lord, I am here to speak with—"

"I said remove it."

The words were quiet. Not barked but measured. It was a command clothed in civility, and somehow all the more dangerous for it.

She ought to have refused. She *wanted* to refuse. But her hands, those traitorous things, had already risen to the buttons. Each one slipped free beneath trembling fingers, and she hated the way her breath hitched as she slid the coat from her shoulders and folded it over one arm. He said nothing as she stood before him, feeling suddenly less armoured than she had in years.

Then he moved.

He stepped forward in a slow and unhurried manner, and she instinctively stepped back. Another step, and she felt the cold firmness of the bookshelf behind her. Her spine straightened, but it was too late to retreat. He stood before her now, tall and uncompromising, so close she could feel the heat radiating from his body. The fire behind him cast the sharp planes of his face in shifting gold and shadow.

"You tremble," he murmured, as his voice curled around her like smoke. "How... odd."

His silver eyes met hers. He was so near. If she lifted her chin even slightly, their mouths would touch. The thought struck her like lightning. It sounded impossible, irrational, and yet she could feel the shape of his breath against her lips.

She could scarcely think. Her pulse roared in her ears. She was never this unmoored, never this unravelled. She could push him away. She *should* push him away. But she didn't.

She stood utterly still, caught in the pull of something she could not name. Every nerve in her body strained towards him. Her hands curled at her sides, aching to reach for him, to steady herself, or perhaps to yield.

Catharine's breath caught as though he had reached inside her chest and drawn it from her lungs with his very own hands. The world had shrunk to this: his eyes, his nearness, the ache blooming low in her belly that no amount of discipline could silence.

"I… came here to talk," she said again, more firmly this time, though the words barely rose above a whisper. Her voice was tight with effort, with the struggle to hold on to reason while every sense betrayed her.

The marquess's eyes didn't waver. "I don't hear you talking."

That was because she never got the chance. The kiss had caught her completely off guard, without warning, without ceremony. It was just the sudden, searing press of his mouth against hers.

Catharine froze, her breath stolen from her lungs. Her mind jolted with the shock of it, for she was not a woman easily caught unaware, but his kiss struck like a match against dry tinder. Heat roared to life inside her.

She should have shoved him away. She should have recoiled, protested, demanded an apology or explanation. But her hands had risen instead to his chest, pushing not with strength but merely resting there, as though testing the solidity of him.

And oh, he *was* solid.

She could feel the breadth of his chest beneath her palms, the thrum of a heartbeat that matched the furious rhythm of her own as his mouth moved against hers, firm and insistent, tasting of brandy and midnight.

There was no gentleness in it. He kissed like a man who had gone too long without softness and no longer believed in such things. He kissed as if it were an act of war, as if he meant to claim something. And the worst part was that she kissed him back.

Her lips parted, and he took it as permission, deepening the kiss with a hunger that stole all air from the room. His hand slid behind her neck, his fingers tangling in her hair as he held her in place, not cruelly but with purpose, with possession. It was intoxicating madness, and yet she never wanted it to end.

That was when a knock shattered the blazing fire. Three crisp raps against the door broke the spell like glass beneath a bootheel. The marquess released her at once, as though scorched.

One moment, his hands were on her, his mouth still near hers, and the next he stepped back with the cold precision of a man returning to the battlefield. All warmth vanished from his face. Only the silver of his eyes remained, narrowed and unreadable.

"Enter!" he shouted, his voice once more that of a marquess, not a man who had just stolen a kiss like a starving thing.

The door creaked open, and a tall, fine-featured woman swept into the room. She was draped in claret silk, every detail of her gown and coiffure designed to command male attention. Her lips were already curled in a coy smile—until they landed on Catharine.

"Oh," the woman said, blinking in confusion. "I wasn't aware... you were already with someone."

The marquess's eyes didn't leave Catharine.

"Yes, I do believe there's been some confusion," she said simply as if it were just a matter of switched parcels.

The marquess' gaze sharpened. "So it seems." He turned to her fully now, distant and assessing. "Who the devil are you?"

The words landed with more force than they should have. He had touched her, no... he had *taken* from her, and now he was looking at her like a puzzle he hadn't meant to pick up.

Catharine met his stare without flinching. "Catharine Fairbourne. I am here on business with you, my lord." Her tone was clipped, as if the heat of his mouth had not just bruised hers.

His jaw visibly ticked. Slowly, he looked to the other woman, who now stood awkwardly near the hearth, watching the two of them like one might observe a duel mid-swing.

"Lady Miriam sent you?" he asked the newcomer.

The woman nodded, her brows lifting. "Of course. I was told the marquess had a need that could be... discreetly handled."

Catharine's stomach turned. The marquess swore under his breath.

He rubbed a hand across his jaw, pacing once, a sharp pivot of boots on hardwood. "Get out."

It was unclear which of them he meant. Catharine didn't wait to find out. She moved to collect her coat. She tried to appear calm and composed, though her fingers shook slightly as she gathered the fabric. Then she swept past the silk-draped woman without a glance.

"Not you," she heard him say, and his voice made her freeze.

Behind her, he spoke again, louder this time, for the other woman's benefit. "You may go. My butler shall see you to the parlour until I resolve this matter. I don't think I shall be long."

The courtesan blinked, her mouth parting in an effort to protest, but the marquess did not deign to look at her again. His attention was fixed entirely on Catharine now, who turned slowly to face him. The other woman hesitated in the doorway once again, evidently in some sort of a rush, but after a tense moment, she gathered her skirts and swept out. The door shut with a decisive click behind her.

"Why didn't you tell me who you were?" he demanded the moment they were alone.

Her fingers tightened on her coat. "You didn't exactly give me time, my lord."

His gaze was unreadable, and his silver eyes were cool and steady. "You could have stopped me, you know."

"Could I?" she replied, sharper than she intended. "You summoned me forward. Told me to remove my coat. Pressed me into a corner and kissed me before I spoke a word. Forgive me if I did not think introductions were welcome."

His jaw clenched, but he didn't deny it.

A long, charged pause passed between them. Then, finally, he spoke again. "Speak now."

Catharine stared at him, her chest rising and falling too fast. She felt undone. Her mind had not caught up to what had just happened, to how close she had come to abandoning every rule she had ever set for herself, and all for a man whose very presence made her body betray her.

She tried to gather her thoughts, to summon the practiced clarity that had served her in every political drawing room and backroom negotiation. But her tongue felt thick, her mouth still warm from his. And though her hands were steady at her sides, her heart pounded with the certainty that whatever this strange, charged thing between them was, it had already begun to rewrite the rules she had lived by her entire life.

And she wasn't sure she knew how to stop it.

Chapter Four

Alaric knew who she was, of course.

Miss Catharine Fairbourne.

He knew the name, though they had never formally met. He'd heard the usual gossip, the tidy labels society gave to women it didn't understand.

The cold spinster. Sharp as a sabre and half as warm.

But nothing in those whispers had prepared him for *her*. And nothing, but truly *nothing,* had prepared him for that kiss. He couldn't find any connection between *that* woman and this reckless fire that met his hunger with her own. But it had been there. Undeniable. Her hands on his chest, the tremble in her breath, the unguarded moment when she gave in.

Alaric knew how to read people. He'd built his entire life on watching for weakness, on sniffing out lies and hidden motives. But what he saw in her unsettled him more than any game of court or war. Because he didn't know what she wanted. And worse, now he didn't know what *he* wanted from her.

"Sit down," he said again, quieter, after he realised she had still not started talking. It was not a command this time but rather a precaution.

She didn't sit. Of course she didn't.

Instead, she merely stepped closer, and that, more than her words, more than even the kiss, was what shook him. Because she was afraid, yes, but not of *him*. Not in the way others were. Her fear was something deeper, more personal, like a woman who'd just found herself staring into a mirror and seeing a stranger reflected back.

He could respect that. He hated how much he *wanted* to.

Shaking the strange thought away, the urge to kiss her again, to abandon reason entirely, Alaric drew in a slow breath and forced his mind back to order and clarity.

Control, damn it.

She stood before him, with her posture composed and her hands folded before her like a diplomat delivering terms of truce. There was no blush now, no wavering, as if the kiss had never happened. And yet he could still feel it on his lips.

Then she cleared her throat softly. "My lord, I come to you with a proposal."

His eyebrow rose in curiosity. "A proposal?"

"Yes." She nodded. "A very simple one, really."

"I'm listening," he replied, feeling a strange sense of patience after the commotion he had just been subject to.

"Marriage."

The word landed like a musket shot. At first, he didn't think he'd heard her right. But there was no possibility of that.

He blinked once. "You mean to tell me—"

"Yes," she interrupted, repeating that word. "Marriage. That is, you and I forming an alliance that would serve us both without the entanglement of emotion."

This was not flirtation. If it were, it would have been the worst attempt he had ever witnessed. But no. This was not some veiled courtship designed to entrap him. Miss Catharine Fairbourne had walked into his house, managed to survive his bad temper and one illicit kiss, and was now offering him the most calculated suggestion of all.

Marriage. Practical. Strategic. *Victimless.*

His jaw tightened.

"Forgive me." He finally found the words. "But that is not a word I hear often. And never quite so... clinically."

"There shall be no romance to speak of," she said briskly, though he caught the faintest tremor at the corner of her mouth. Uncertainty, perhaps? Or pride, she was daring him to strike down. "It is merely a matter of alliance."

"Between us?"

"Yes. Your title and reach. My family's influence. Particularly, my father's recent association with the Duke of Kingswell."

Alaric narrowed his eyes. *Damn.* That was clever. Kingswell had the ear of half the lords in the North *and* a private army the Crown pretended not to notice. A marriage to the Fairbourne family would plant Alaric squarely in the centre of that web, especially now that he was slipping from favour.

It all sounded convenient, dangerous... tempting.

"And your father... he knows of this scheme?" he asked, more curious than cautious.

She shook her head once. "No. Nor will he. He's more concerned with my usefulness, not how I'm placed."

There was a hard edge to those words. It was not bitterness, though. He doubted she allowed herself the luxury. It was simply the truth. She knew her value in political currency, and she'd long ago resigned herself to it.

He exhaled, pacing once towards the fire. Everything in him wanted to say no. On principle, of course. Or perhaps on instinct. The thing was, he didn't trust easy answers, and he trusted beautiful, self-possessed women offering convenient marriages even less.

But this wasn't convenient. Not really. This was something else. Something calculated, cold, and perhaps... a mirror of himself.

"You'd marry a scarred, battle-worn marquess," he said finally, "to give your family leverage?"

She looked him straight in the eye. "Yes."

"You *wouldn't* marry for affection?"

That made her hesitate for the first time since she had appeared before him. Then she glanced away, just for a breath.

"No," she said softly. "That's not a luxury I believe in."

Ah. So... that was it.

He stepped closer, not touching her. No. He didn't dare do that again on the same night. But he was close enough that she had to feel the heat off him, the sheer weight of his presence.

"Let's be clear, Miss Fairbourne," he said with his mind buzzing with the fury of a million bees. "If I agree to this, it won't be a fiction. You'll live here. You'll be bound to me by law and title. You'll have to endure the whispers. The blood on my hands, the truths most men keep buried."

"I'm not afraid of scandal," she said quickly.

"Evidently not, otherwise you wouldn't be here in the middle of the night," he murmured, remembering the gossip. "But are you afraid of *me*?"

A pause. Her eyes met his. "Yes."

The honesty struck him clean through the ribs. *Good*. He didn't want her naïve. And now she was offering herself in the one form he might actually accept. She was offering an alliance, a shared war, with a woman who was as sharp and as broken as he was.

"You should have the documents prepared," she said, her voice once again composed. "The terms will be straightforward. No title claims beyond what is legally owed. And I will not interfere in your household. All I require is that you are ready for marriage in two days."

"Two days?" His eyes widened in disbelief.

"Yes," she replied calmly. "As I've said, this is a business arrangement and shall be treated as such. The urgency is part of the contract."

"Well, you've certainly made it unromantic enough to tempt me," Alaric muttered, more to himself than her.

One of her brows lifted slightly. "Was that intended as a complaint?"

He huffed a quiet breath. It felt like something between amusement and disbelief. "No. A compliment, oddly."

She didn't smile. He hadn't expected her to.

"Fine," he agreed, feeling strangely relieved and equally apprehensive, a combination he rarely acknowledged. "I'll visit Fairbourne House tomorrow to speak with your father."

Catharine nodded once, as if confirming that a trade route had been opened or an alliance secured. "He'll be surprised but not disapproving. You're too valuable a piece on the board for him to protest."

"Charming."

"I am certain that you want honesty from me."

Alaric tilted his head. "To be quite honest, I want to know who I'm marrying."

"You already do," she said to remind him of the gossip again. "Just as I know what I'm agreeing to."

He said nothing to that. There was nothing to say. She was right.

"I shall wait for you tomorrow afternoon. Father will be gone until noon," she added, stepping back at last, drawing on her gloves as though this were any ordinary business transaction.

He watched her cross to the door, every step measured and sure. There was no fluster, no backward glance. Just before she reached for the latch, she paused.

And then, glancing at him sidelong, she commented, "This was easily the strangest proposal I've ever heard of."

"God help me," Alaric muttered, "it's the only one I've ever accepted."

She inclined her head. "Then we're even."

And with that, Miss Catharine Fairbourne opened the door and vanished into the darkened corridor, her footsteps vanishing like smoke. Alaric stood motionless in the centre of the room, still holding his half-finished glass of brandy. The room suddenly felt too quiet, too large. Too... empty.

He exhaled slowly and dragged a hand down his scarred jaw, the skin pulling tight beneath his palm.

I am getting married.

To a woman who had just accused him of kissing her into silence. And then offered herself, not in apology or passion, but as a tactical alliance.

"I need a stronger drink," he muttered, returning to the sideboard.

Of all the absurdities he'd witnessed in his life, such as dukes plotting in dark corners, spies turning traitor for a whisper of gold, and noblemen dressing up their pet pigs and entering them into garden competitions, *this* had officially taken the bloody prize.

He downed the rest of his brandy in one go. He stared into the fire for a moment longer, the empty glass heavy in his hand. And then—*damn it all*—he remembered.

The other woman.

She was still waiting patiently in the parlour, no doubt rehearsing some sultry line she'd been coached to deliver. His jaw clenched as the absurdity of the night reached its final note.

He strode to the door, yanked it open, and summoned his butler with a sharp "Langley."

The man appeared with his usual ghostlike efficiency, blinking up at him with professional calm. "My lord?"

"The woman in the parlour... tell her she's been dismissed."

Langley's expression didn't flicker. "Of course, my lord."

"Yes. Tell her..." Alaric exhaled hard through his nose, pinching the bridge of it. "Tell her I've had a change in priorities."

"As you wish."

"And pay her," Alaric added. "A full evening's fee, plus whatever insult her pride will require. I don't want any whispers finding their way to Lady Miriam."

Langley inclined his head. "Very well, my lord."

"One more thing." Alaric turned back as the butler moved to depart. "Tell the young lady to convey a message to Lady Miriam directly."

Langley waited.

"Let her know," Alaric said coldly, "that I won't be needing her services any longer."

"Shall I express that... diplomatically?"

"Use whatever words you like," Alaric said, stepping back into his study.

Langley nodded once more and vanished down the corridor like a shadow swallowed by dusk.

Alaric closed the door behind him and stood in the centre of the room again, feeling the silence press in from all sides. The air still smelled faintly of brandy, wax, and *her*. It was the scent of something subtle and cold and maddeningly elusive, like snow clinging to stone.

He looked towards the hearth. The flames crackled quietly.

Marriage.

To a woman who didn't flinch at his scar, or blink at the rumours, or ask him for anything but terms.

It was ludicrous. It was transactional. It was *precisely* the sort of thing he should have rejected outright. Instead, he was going to marry her.

He thought of how she had looked at him. There was no simpering, no feigned horror, no nervous glances at the scar that cleaved his face. That alone was intriguing. But intrigue did not win seats, nor silence the vultures in Parliament. However, a marriage to such a woman might.

It was not sentiment that stirred within him. Alaric had little left for sentiment. What he possessed was calculation. This was a move. A bold, visible one. The union of a war-scarred peer and a young lady of good breeding. It might be enough to force the ton to reconsider its whispers, to force the clubs to temper their jeers.

Her respectability would reflect upon him like borrowed sunlight, softening the shadow that clung to his name. The House of Lords could sneer, but they could not ignore a man with renewed alliances and a bride at his side.

The truth was, he needed allies. Votes. She might give him both. The marriage would be a signal to his enemies, to the press, to the idle bastards who clinked their glasses and called him a beast behind his back.

Well, let them try and do so to her face. He knew that they would not dare.

He reached for the decanter again.

What was stranger still? He didn't regret it.

Not yet, anyway...

Chapter Five

"Who are we waiting for, Catharine?"

Catharine turned sharply from the window, the hem of her gown whispering across the drawing room carpet as she paced. "No one you need to concern yourself with."

Margaret, curled like a cat in the corner chair, frowned and tilted her head. "You've been pacing for the better part of an hour. That's quite a long time for no one of importance."

"I'm expecting a caller," Catharine replied crisply, though her voice held a thread of tension she couldn't quite iron out. "A man... but it's truly no one *that* important."

Margaret sat up straighter, blue eyes widening with sudden, eager interest. "A gentleman caller? My heavens, who? Why didn't you tell me?"

"Because it truly doesn't matter." Catharine tried to seem disinterested, but she was obviously failing spectacularly at it. "It is merely... a favour."

"A favour?" her sister repeated. "For whom?"

"Oh, really, Margaret... what is the point of all these questions?" Catharine pouted, turning away.

Margaret huffed, rising and flouncing towards the settee like a heroine in a rather dramatic play. "You know, if you aim to be mysterious, you should be much more charming about it."

Catharine heard the playful overtones of the comment, but she chose not to answer. Her eyes drifted back to the window.

She was never nervous. She was deliberate, rational, composed. Her actions were always weighed, her decisions methodical. Every piece in her life was selected and placed as if on a chessboard.

But today... Today was the day after she had kissed a man before offering him her hand in marriage, as if it were a business contract.

Dear God, what have I done?

She pressed her fingers to her temples, willing the thoughts into silence.

Margaret's voice broke through again, much softer now. "Catharine... is something wrong?"

"No," she replied quickly. Too quickly.

"You're pale."

"I'm *always* pale."

"You're trembling."

"I am *cold*, Margaret." She folded her arms tightly across her chest, more to stop the fluttering inside her than anything visible.

Margaret crossed to her, gently touching her arm. "You look like a woman waiting for the guillotine."

"Don't be dramatic."

"Then tell me what this is." Margaret's tone turned uncharacteristically serious. "Is someone forcing you to do something?"

"No." Catharine's voice turned sharp. "No one forces me. Ever."

Strangely enough, that much was true. Even now. *Especially* now.

Then the carriage wheels sounded outside. The gravel crunched, and hooves struck a rhythm across the stones. Her heart lurched once, hard and fast, as if her body had realised before her mind that it was too late to undo what she'd set in motion.

He was here, and he was a dark figure who stepped down from the black carriage in the drive. He looked taller than she remembered. Broader, somehow. The wind tugged at his coat as he glanced up at the house, and for one fleeting moment, he seemed to meet her eyes through the glass.

Catharine swallowed hard. This was no longer a plan. This was a storm. She paced about the room nervously, wondering what would be the best position to welcome him. Standing? Sitting down? Did it even matter?

She had no idea how much time had passed, but the drawing room door finally opened.

"Lord Ravensedge, Miss Fairbourne," the butler announced with quiet gravity.

Catharine turned slowly as Lord Ravensedge stepped into the room.

She had thought herself prepared. She had not been.

In the stark clarity of daylight, he looked larger than memory allowed. His shoulders filled the dark lines of his coat, and his presence was as heavy as thunderclouds. The jagged scar that carved a path from temple to jaw had no candlelight to soften it now. It stood in brutal contrast against the sharp symmetry of his other features, lending him the look of a man carved not by God but by war.

At that same moment, Catharine's father entered the drawing room, his eyes traversing the faces of everyone present, recognizing his two daughters momentarily but widening at the sight of the unexpected visitor.

"Lord Ravensedge," Catharine's father greeted stiffly. "You... honour us."

Lord Ravensedge inclined his head in that particular way he had. "Lord Fairbourne."

Margaret, standing just behind their father, seemed to forget her manners entirely. Her blue eyes widened, mouth slightly agape, as though she'd stumbled into the pages of a gothic novel.

Catharine stepped forward, her voice cutting into the tension like a blade. "May I present my younger sister, Miss Margaret Fairbourne."

Lord Ravensedge's silver gaze flicked to the girl. "Miss Margaret."

Margaret managed a curtsey that was more awe than etiquette. "My lord."

Lord Fairbourne motioned stiffly to the chairs. "Shall we sit?"

They did, while the silence reigned among them.

"I've come to make my intentions known," Lord Ravensedge announced without hesitation. "I've come to ask for Catharine's hand."

Lord Fairbourne blinked. "I... see."

"Under usual circumstances," he continued, "I suspect such a proposal might warrant more courtship. But these are not usual circumstances. I believe Miss Fairbourne and I are both of the view that practicality must take precedence."

Catharine studied her father's face. He looked deeply unsettled. Not angry but thrown off balance, as though the very idea of someone pursuing his eldest daughter under these circumstances was foreign. Which, to be fair, it was.

"You'll forgive me, Lord Ravensedge," her father said slowly, "but I was not aware the two of you had... an understanding."

"We don't," Lord Ravensedge said.

That single word dropped like a stone.

Her father's brow furrowed. "Then why—?"

"Because I am in need of a wife, and she is in need of a husband."

It was an explanation that should have sounded insulting. But from his mouth, it rang with brutal clarity.

"Catharine?" her father said, turning to her now, voice thin with disbelief.

She nodded, her chin lifting a fraction. "We've come to a mutual arrangement, Father."

"Also, I have no need of a dowry," Lord Ravensedge added. "My wealth is considerable. From what I understand, you have the entire wedding already set up. It would be a shame for it all to go to waste."

Her father's jaw worked silently for a moment.

Margaret blinked between them. "This is all very... very sudden."

"It's already done," Catharine said simply.

Her father shook his head. "You make it sound like a treaty, not a match."

"It is a kind of treaty," Lord Ravensedge said, folding one gloved hand over the other. "Catharine is not the sort of woman who requires trinkets and poetry. She has sense. I, for one, find it refreshing."

That silenced the room again.

Catharine's father stood up soundlessly, approaching the hearth. He rested his hand atop the carved wooden mantelpiece, almost as if he were in need of something to steady him. Lord Ravensedge followed suit, standing up.

"Why don't I give you a moment to discuss things privately?" he suggested. "I shall be outside, in the garden, waiting for Miss Fairbourne to join me."

Catharine watched her father nod, after which Lord Ravensedge gave a small bow of the head and disappeared out the door. She remained standing with her spine straight and her fingers folded tightly before her. She felt like she was being assessed, and she knew her father did not like the sum.

"Ravensedge," her father began, glancing towards the door, "is a... man of reputation. A difficult one, perhaps. His political entanglements are not unknown to me. Nor are his... scars."

Catharine's jaw clenched.

"He's not what I expected," her father continued, his voice more careful now, as if testing each word. "I had always assumed that... well, someone of a quieter disposition might suit you better."

She narrowed her eyes. "Someone less visible, you mean."

Her father looked uncomfortable. "Only that your... temperament has never encouraged great speculation."

"And now it has."

He flinched slightly at her tone, then he tried again. "Catharine, you are aware of what such a match entails? Ravensedge is not an easy man. There are whispers, of course, and—"

"And none of them concern you unless I become a scandal," she said coolly. "Isn't that right?"

He stiffened. "That isn't fair."

"No?" Her voice sharpened, quiet but cutting. "You wanted me married. You wanted to see me settled, useful, spoken for. And now you have it. A marquess, no less. Title, fortune, alliances… he checks every box you've silently kept for the past six years."

Her father didn't speak. He only looked at her in a way that made him appear weathered and worn.

Catharine pressed forward with a final edge to her voice. "This is what should make you happy, Father. My marriage. So be happy."

The silence that followed was loud and leaden. Lord Fairbourne stared at his daughter for a long, long moment, and then he looked away, as though her words had landed too precisely for comfort. His shoulders sagged, just slightly. Then he finally nodded.

"Very well," he said. "I'll see to the settlements."

That was all. There was no blessing, no warmth. Just the business of a father done with his duty. Catharine drew in a breath, steeling her voice against the tremor that threatened to slip in.

"Now, if there is nothing else," she said evenly, "I will go into the garden to discuss the final particulars of my marriage with the man I have chosen to be my husband. The man who, as it happens, will also preserve this family from further embarrassment."

Her father blinked at her but said nothing. His eyes were unreadable, as though he'd already washed his hands of whatever cost this bargain might extract from her.

She held his gaze for a heartbeat longer, foolishly hoping that he might say something... anything. That he might show some small sign that he saw what this truly meant. That she was laying down the last of her pride, her hope, her heart, for the sake of the family name.

But he merely gave a shallow nod and turned away. *That*, Catharine thought bitterly, *is answer enough.*

When she turned to go, her eyes caught on Margaret, who was still standing by the door, her expression pale and hollow with shock. The usual spark in her eyes had dulled to silence. For once, her sister had nothing to say.

Catharine felt that silence like a hand around her throat. Even Margaret couldn't speak. The bright, impulsive, golden Margaret had no words to share. That could only mean one thing, and that was that the truth was plain. There was no one coming to stop her. There was no one coming to save her.

So she straightened her spine, turned without a word, and walked from the drawing room with the slow, deliberate grace of a woman being led to her own execution.

The corridor was cool and quiet, and outside, the sky was overcast, the pale grey light offering little warmth. A wind stirred the garden hedges as she stepped down the stone path, each movement rehearsed in her mind, though none of it felt real.

She found him near the rose arch. Lord Ravensedge was standing with one gloved hand resting lightly on the back of a stone bench, his silver-grey eyes turned towards the distant trees, as if he, too, had grown weary of walls and expectations. His profile was stark against the shifting clouds, all too scarred and severe yet somehow steady in a way that made the ground beneath her feet feel less certain.

He turned as she approached, his gaze sweeping over her face in silence.

"I presume we are to speak now," she said, keeping her voice carefully neutral.

He nodded once. "It seems we are."

Chapter Six

"I want clarity between us," he heard her say, breaking the silence. "I harbour no illusions, no romantic fancies. This is a union of utility, and I will not be an ornament."

He resisted the urge to smile. "I would be insulted if you tried."

"You may take your affairs where you will," she said, though her voice thinned with the words. "Discretion is all I ask."

"I have no time for affairs," he said flatly. "And no interest in starting one."

He noticed the way his answer struck her. Perhaps she hadn't been expecting it.

She looked away, staring out across the tangled hedgerows.

"I'm aware," she said at last, quietly, "that I am no one's first choice. Twice shunned. I know how people speak of me."

Alaric watched her in silence for a long moment after she'd spoken.

The wind lifted a strand of her dark hair, tugging it loose from its careful pins. She didn't notice. Or perhaps she did and simply didn't care. He found that he liked that about her, how still she stood in the wind, unyielding. There was something about Catharine Fairbourne that reminded him of winter stone: cold, yes, but shaped by time and force, therefore making it unbreakable.

It was not what he'd expected. But then, nothing about her had been.

He reached into the inner pocket of his coat and drew out the small, velvet-covered box he'd pocketed before leaving his townhouse. The ring inside had belonged to his grandmother. It was not ornate. There was no delicate filigree or fluttering diamonds. It was just a thick gold band with a single emerald set in its centre, deep green, almost black in low light. He held it out between them.

"For the sake of appearances," he said in a matter-of-fact manner.

She looked down at it without reaching. "You carry heirlooms casually, my lord."

He shrugged one shoulder. "The role of husband seemed to require one. I don't enjoy improvising."

She took the ring without ceremony, her fingers grazing his only briefly. A flicker of heat passed through him at the contact, unwanted and unwelcome. He said nothing.

Her eyes lifted to his. "What precisely do *you* expect of *me*?"

"Public civility." He replied with the first thing that popped into his mind. "No scandal. No romantic declarations. We play our roles, nothing more. You'll manage the household and the social obligations. I will manage the estates and political affairs."

"And privacy?" she asked.

"You'll have it. My staff will answer to you once the marriage is complete. You'll have full freedom of the London house and the Ravensedge estate. So long as you don't set fire to either, I will not interfere."

Her brow arched slightly. "How generous."

Alaric met her gaze, cool and unwavering. "I'm not offering you a cage, Catharine. Just a contract, which, if I recall, you came to me with. We'll be allies. Nothing more."

She nodded once, slipping the ring onto her finger without a glance downward. "Then allow me to be plain as well. I don't intend to be anyone's pawn. If I suspect I am being lied to or used for ends not agreed upon, I will not sit quietly."

"I wouldn't expect you to."

The corners of her mouth shifted, somewhere between a smirk and the ghost of a frown. It was the closest she'd come to smiling.

"We must make it believable," he said after a pause. "At least in public. People will be watching. And also questioning."

Her eyes lingered on his for a moment too long. "Then we'd best learn to look convincing."

Alaric inclined his head slightly, though something inside him tightened at her words.

Convincing. That was the key to all of it. *Lie well. Smile better. Pretend until truth forgets what it looked like.*

He had lived like that for years. What was one more performance?

And yet, as she turned her hand, examining the emerald on her finger, he found himself struck by how quiet the moment was.

Not a declaration. Not a proposal. Not even a promise.

Just a transaction. Silent and binding. And somehow, that seemed to make it feel far more dangerous, even as he looked at the ring on her finger, nestled as if it had always belonged there. That, he found, was the unsettling part: not how easily she wore it but how right it looked. As though fate had decided long ago to pull them together, not for love but for something sharper, more dangerous.

He let out a breath and straightened his coat. "I will meet you at the church," he said.

She didn't blink. Merely inclined her head as though sealing a business arrangement. There was no softening in her eyes, no dreamy nerves, no naïve flutter of a girl caught in the whirlwind of a wedding. Just cold, ruthless clarity. Alaric recognised it because he wore the same thing behind his own gaze.

He gave a short nod, then turned away. The wind caught the edge of his greatcoat as he walked back across the garden path. He didn't look back.

That wasn't the sort of arrangement they had.

***

Catharine waited until he was completely out of sight before she allowed herself to exhale. The ring felt foreign on her hand. In fact, it felt heavier than gold had any right to be.

She turned it once, twice, then curled her fingers into a fist.

No time to think about it now. No time to feel.

She crossed the garden in measured strides, slipping back into the house through the servants' corridor, hoping to bypass the drawing room entirely. If she could reach the staircase unseen, she might have a few precious hours to herself—time to sit alone, perhaps, and remember how to breathe. But as she neared the front hall, the drawing room door flew open with theatrical force.

"Catharine!"

Margaret appeared in the doorway, cheeks flushed and eyes wide, her pale gold curls in gentle disarray. The expression on her face was halfway between relief and panic.

"I've been waiting for you for ages," she said, rushing forward. "What took you so long? What did he say? Are you mad?"

"I don't have time for this," Catharine muttered, brushing past her.

Margaret followed, undeterred. "You agreed to marry him? Just like that? He's... he's grim, Catharine! He hardly said a word. And did you see his face?"

Catharine stopped mid-step and turned.

Margaret faltered at once, but her voice didn't lose its edge. "I'm not trying to be cruel, but... that scar. It's... he's frightening."

Of course, Margaret would fixate on the visible wound. The one the world whispered about. The one that turned heads and ended conversations. It was easier than asking what it meant to live behind a face like that. Or beside it.

"Is that truly all you see?" Catharine asked quietly.

Margaret blinked in surprise. "What else is there to see?"

Catharine looked away.

Margaret stepped forward, more tentative now. "You barely know him. He's older, distant... and you're you. You could wait for someone else. You don't have to do this."

Catharine's smile was thin and humourless. "Don't I?"

The silence that followed was louder than anything Margaret could have said. For a moment, she looked like she might cry. But even she understood, on some unspoken level, that the decision had already been taken.

Catharine's voice, when it came again, was colder than before.

"This is not a storybook, Margaret. There is no prince coming. There is no perfect match. There is survival and reputation... and consequences."

"But—"

"This is what Father wants," Catharine interrupted. "Isn't that what matters? His name. His legacy. His shameful daughter finally off his hands."

Margaret recoiled, stricken.

Immediately, Catharine regretted the sharpness. But she couldn't take it back. Not now. Not when everything inside her had already calcified into something hard enough to carry her through tomorrow. Without another word, she turned and walked past her sister, leaving the scent of the garden and Margaret's stunned silence behind her.

Moments later, she closed the door to her chambers with a careful click. The sound echoed like finality.

She stood for a moment with her back against the wood, staring at nothing, her breath shallow and uneven in her chest. The quiet pressed in, offering no distraction, no escape. Her body felt distant, as though weighed down by invisible chains.

Slowly, she moved across the room, and there it was.

The wedding gown.

It hung from the screen near her window, bathed in the last grey light of day. It was soft silk in a pale shade of ivory... clean, uncreased, untouched. The lace along the bodice had been stitched by hand. The delicate embroidery at the hem traced blooming garden roses, painstakingly chosen for their elegance.

It had been made for another man. Another future.

Catharine stared at it, her throat tightening. She had once let herself believe she might wear it with joy. Foolish, romantic hope, quickly extinguished, of course. Reality had seen to that. But still, there had been a time, albeit brief and breathless, when she'd stood before this very gown and wondered what it would be like to walk down an aisle with her heart still whole.

Her lips trembled despite herself. She pressed them shut, for this wasn't about dresses or the scarred man who would be waiting at the church. It was about the shape of her life, how every path had narrowed until only this one remained. She had chosen it, yes, with all the calculation she possessed. But now, stripped of strategy, she was left with something colder.

Her hands clenched at her sides. She wanted to be certain. She had always been certain. But now...right now, the mirror refused to lie for her.

She sat at the edge of her bed, staring down at the bare floorboards. Her thoughts swirled without form. Her chest ached in a way that had nothing to do with heartbreak and everything to do with endurance.

This marriage would save her family. It would save her name. It would be a ticket to her sister's bright future. But most importantly, it would cost her something she could never ask for back.

Tomorrow, she would put on the dress. She would meet a man she barely knew and become his wife. Not for love. Not for hope. But because there was no other choice left to her.

Catharine rose once more and crossed to the window. Outside, the garden was bathed in the last light of the dying sun. She touched the pane with one hand, cold meeting cold.

Tomorrow. She whispered it to herself like a prayer.

Then she turned back to the dress.

Chapter Seven

"God help me, you look like you're going to your execution."

Alaric didn't flinch as his cousin, Lady Isadora Vale, swept into the room without so much as a knock, a rustle of crimson silk and foreign perfume announcing her presence before her voice did.

He buttoned the cuff of his coat with deliberate precision. "You're early."

"I travelled across the bloody country to arrive in time," she said lightly. "You're lucky I didn't bring an orchestra."

She crossed to the window, threw open the curtains, and let in the grey, reluctant light of morning. Alaric winced. His head ached. His cravat was too tight. His boots had never felt heavier. Isadora, of course, noticed everything.

"My dear cousin, you look absolutely miserable," she said, turning to face him with a raised brow. "And you haven't even seen the bride yet."

"I've seen her."

"Have you?" Isadora tilted her head, amusement flickering in her dark eyes. "Then perhaps you'll explain why you're tying that cravat as if preparing for a duel."

Alaric sighed. "I've told you already. I don't have time for dramatics this morning."

"Oh, darling," she said, gliding across the room and plucking the cravat from his hands. "Then you really shouldn't have invited me to the wedding."

"I didn't."

She grinned. "Details."

Alaric let her retie the knot, though he didn't meet her eyes. Isadora was many things. She was vain, brilliant, entirely too observant, but never sentimental. She hadn't set foot in London in five years, not since her husband had finally done the decent thing and died. Alaric had almost forgotten what it felt like to be under the lens of someone who could read him as easily as a ledger.

"You truly mean to go through with it, then?" she asked quietly, tightening the cloth with practiced fingers. "Marrying the spinster with the formidable eyebrows?"

"Yes."

"No scandal? No war of houses? Just a quiet ceremony and a practical arrangement?" She stepped back to inspect her work, then met his gaze squarely. "How... unromantic."

Alaric's mouth curled into something resembling a smile. "Romance is for fools."

"Then I imagine you're precisely her type."

He laughed. "She's clever. Cold. Disciplined to the bone."

Isadora arched a brow. "And you admire that?"

"I understand it."

Isadora walked to the chair by the hearth, lowered herself with the grace of someone born to command a room, and folded one leg over the other.

"You don't think she'll come to regret it?" she asked, and this time her voice was softer, edged in something almost like concern.

"She already regrets it," Alaric said, fastening his waistcoat. "That's what makes her dangerous."

He crossed to the looking glass, adjusted the lapel of his coat, and stared at the reflection before him. He looked every inch the marquess. Imposing. Composed. Ready for war.

"You always did have a taste for impossible women," Isadora said behind him.

He didn't answer.

After a moment, she rose and crossed to his side, resting a gloved hand lightly on his shoulder. Their eyes met in the glass.

"Don't punish her for being what you like about her," she said quietly. "Even you deserve something that feels real."

Then, without waiting for a reply, she kissed his cheek and swept out of the room in a swirl of silk and irreverence.

Alaric stood alone again, the silence pressing in once more. The church bells would toll soon... and they did.

The church was stifling.

Though the morning air was crisp outside, within the stone walls of St. James', the warmth of too many bodies and the buzz of barely veiled curiosity made the space feel claustrophobic.

Whispers floated beneath the organ music like smoke: *A sudden engagement... She had been jilted... Why her? Why him? Did he need funds? Did she?*

Alaric stood at the altar, tall and still as a statue cut from iron. His expression betrayed nothing, though his eyes swept the crowd with clinical detachment. They were all there, the vultures in silk and satin, eager to witness a spectacle. Some smirked. Some gossiped behind fans. He knew the way they looked at him: the scar, the shadowed past, the rumors. And now the jilted bride. They couldn't have written a more delicious scandal.

Let them look.

Then the hush came. A collective turn of heads. She had arrived.

Catharine Fairbourne stepped into the aisle with her father on one arm and her sisters close behind. Her gown was not overly elaborate. In fact, it was simple in cut but exquisite in detail. Ivory silk with a high waist and long sleeves, embroidered delicately along the hems and cuffs. There was no sparkle, no excess. Just the elegant restraint of a woman who knew exactly what she was offering the world... and what she wasn't.

Her face was composed, her spine impossibly straight. In the daylight, her beauty was not the type that softened. No, it sharpened. She had the kind of face one remembered in full, not in fragments. Every line precise. Every glance measured. She wasn't smiling.

And yet there was something about her. It struck him again, like it had in the study. That strange, quiet pull beneath his ribs. It wasn't her figure, though he'd noticed it. Not her face, though it was finely drawn. It was something more dangerous. Something in her self-possession. The way she dared to walk into a room full of wolves and not flinch.

He didn't move as she reached him, didn't offer a smile or a bow. Their eyes met just for a second and held.

That was when the priest began. The ceremony unfolded with the solemn rhythm of duty, each word a step further into permanence. Vows were exchanged. Rings followed. Her voice was steady when she spoke. His was unwavering. They did not touch except as required. When he slid the ring onto her finger, her hand was cool. When she did the same, her fingers brushed his just slightly... whether on purpose or by accident, he couldn't tell.

But he felt it. Every second of it. He wondered, distantly, if she did too.

"You may kiss the bride," came the priest's voice, weighty and final.

Alaric turned to her. The room held its breath. Catharine inclined her chin barely perceptibly, but it was permission, nonetheless.

He stepped forward and kissed her. It was nothing like the first kiss. His lips pressed to hers with the solemnity of a pact, not the heat of desire. When he pulled back, her eyes had not closed. She looked at him not like a wife. Not like a stranger. But like a match to a fuse.

And somewhere deep in his chest, he felt the first flicker of fire.

The church erupted in polite applause. With Catharine at his side, Alaric headed out of the chapel, feeling the curious and cruel gazes alike buzzing around them like hornets. He ignored them. Isadora, of course, did not.

As he guided Catharine down the chapel steps, his cousin lingered behind, elegantly cornered by a cluster of acquaintances. She wore widow's black with a scarlet sash, and her eyes sparkled with mischief as she deflected questions with a rapier wit only she possessed.

"Lord Ravensedge does tend to surprise us all," she said airily. "Especially when he chooses to marry a woman with a brain. Scandalous, isn't it?"

Alaric heard her, of course. Isadora had never learned to whisper. But he didn't look back. Catharine was silent beside him, walking in precise and measured steps as the train of her gown trailed behind like a banner of surrender. Or defiance... he hadn't decided yet.

As they approached the carriage, a footman sprang to attention. Alaric helped her inside, then followed, settling beside her in the dim, enclosed space. The door shut with a solid thud. Then silence.

The horses lurched forward, and London began to roll past the windows: grey stone, soot-streaked glass, the faceless blur of bystanders. Inside the carriage, the hush was almost oppressive. Catharine sat with her posture that of a queen, prepared to be judged by lesser beings. Her hands, gloved in soft cream kid, rested lightly in her lap, unmoving.

She didn't speak. Neither did he.

It was not an awkward silence but a calculated one. They were like two generals seated on opposite ends of a battlefield, neither willing to reveal the first crack in armour.

This woman, this stranger who now bore his name, wasn't easily shaken. But she was shaken now. He could feel it, the same way he could sense the tension in a horse before a storm.

The carriage wheels clattered over cobblestones. A sharp turn jostled them briefly, and his shoulder brushed hers. She didn't flinch. She didn't move at all. That was how she remained through the wedding breakfast that followed as well.

Ravensedge Hall had seen grander occasions. Isadora's first season ball came to mind, as did his father's funeral, but Alaric had made it clear: no excessive fanfare, no intrusive spectacle. Just a modest assembly of relatives, a few necessary acquaintances, and a menu chosen for taste, not pomp.

The drawing room had been set with quiet elegance: pale linen, fresh greenery, and the old family silver polished until it caught every flicker of candlelight. The air carried the scents of roasted capon, lemon syllabub, and tension.

He stood near the mantelpiece with a glass of claret untouched in his hand and watched her.

Miss Catharine Fairbourne—Lady Ravensedge now—moved through the room like a chess master surveying the board. Every word she spoke was deliberate, and every glance was purposeful. She did not fidget or falter. Even now, mere hours after marrying a man she barely knew, she looked entirely unshakeable.

But he saw it. It truly wasn't much, just a momentary stillness when her father approached. It was a slight lift of her shoulders. It was the steel behind her civility when one of Isadora's acquaintances muttered something thinly veiled about *a most unconventional match.*

Catharine responded with a smile so crisp it could slice fruit, and oddly enough, he found himself amused. And more than a little intrigued.

At that moment, Isadora swept to his side, a wineglass in one hand and a sardonic glint in her eye.

"She's magnificent," his cousin murmured without any congratulations prior to her words. "You've married a statue carved by a particularly haughty Roman."

Alaric didn't look away from Catharine. "I'm almost certain that she speaks Latin better than you."

Isadora gave a soft, wicked laugh. "God help you, Alaric. You may have just married someone who outmanoeuvres you."

"She's not playing a game."

Isadora arched a brow. "Then why do you look like a man trying not to lose one?"

He didn't answer. Instead, he moved through the room, nodding once to a viscount he barely tolerated, brushing off a dowager's attempt to reminisce about his mother, until he found Catharine standing near the long windows with a glass in hand, speaking quietly with her sister.

Margaret Fairbourne looked as though she had been crying. Catharine's posture was gentle but firm as she leaned in closer and whispered something into Margaret's ear. Several moments later, Catharine was alone, and Alaric couldn't resist seizing the chance to speak to her.

"Lord Ravensedge," she greeted, her tone formal but not cold.

"Lady Ravensedge," he returned, just as evenly. "You've managed them well."

"I'm not sure *managed* is the word I'd use." She glanced back at the guests. "But I'm practiced at enduring long conversations with shallow intentions."

"Ah." He nodded. "A truly useful talent."

She didn't smile. "I imagine we'll be requiring a number of useful talents in the weeks ahead."

There it was again. That iron sense of purpose beneath her civility. The sense that she was bracing for war while dressed for dinner.

He inclined his head. "You've made an impression."

"I'm aware."

"Not all of them kind."

"I didn't marry to be admired."

Alaric studied her for a long moment, then offered the following words without thinking. "There's still time to change your mind."

Her brow lifted a fraction. "You say that now, after the ink is dry and the gossip printed."

His mouth twitched. "I'm told I lack tact."

"I'd call it directness. Not always unwelcome."

A pause passed between them. He didn't know what he expected her to say next. Perhaps a request to retire early or a cutting remark about the arrangement they had just sealed, but instead, her words took him by surprise.

"You'll let me know when it's time to perform affection."

He blinked. "Perform?"

"In public. When appearances require it. I assume you'd prefer to avoid surprises."

He set his glass down on a nearby table. "You think I'd be surprised if you touched me?"

"Well, you'll have to endure touching me as well," she pointed out.

That landed with more weight than he'd expected. For a moment, he saw not the bride in pearls and silk but the woman beneath it: tired, resolute, and infinitely alone.

"I don't expect you to endure me," he said at last.

"Then we are already ahead of most marriages."

She turned then and left him with the distant scent of lavender and a silence he couldn't quite name.

Chapter Eight

That night, when everything had come to an end, or better yet, when their true beginning was to commence, Catharine walked beside Lord Ravensedge, her husband, even as tension coiled in the pit of her stomach.

She should not be nervous. She had agreed to this. She had even orchestrated it, this union of mutual benefit. She was not some naïve girl with petals still clinging to her lashes. She had known precisely what she was doing when she made the offer. And yet...

He suddenly paused before a tall oak door carved with the Vale crest. Without a word, he opened it and stood aside, allowing her to pass through.

"Lady Ravensedge," he said simply.

Her throat worked as she nodded and stepped into the room.

The chamber was enormous, warmed by the soft glow of a hearth that crackled gently with fresh logs. The bed dominated the space, as it ought to do in a bedchamber. It was high, canopied in cream and deep blue silk, with the curtains half-drawn.

A fire's light played along its posts. To the left, tall windows offered a view of the darkened garden, veiled in moonlight. A low table held decanters and crystal. And in the far corner, almost hidden, there was a second door, discreet and closed for the time being. She could only assume that it was the adjoining chamber.

He closed the door behind them with a soft click. She turned.

He was watching her. Not coldly, not kindly either, but with the same measured, piercing gaze he had worn all day. That was the gaze that unsettled her. It stripped things bare.

"I've had your maid sent for," he said at last. "You may take your time."

Her fingers twitched at her side. "Thank you."

He crossed to the small table and poured himself a measure of something dark and amber. "You're uncomfortable."

She hesitated. "Only uncertain."

He sipped, then set the glass down without drinking more. "Understandable." He didn't come closer. Instead, he just stood beyond the reach of firelight. "After what we've both… endured today, I would leave you alone, but I'm afraid that we must make this marriage look completely and utterly real to those around us."

She swallowed heavily. "Appearances?"

"Yes." He met her gaze. "There are always eyes. Servants talk. Gentry listen. Every glance, every absence, every whisper will be noted now. If they sense this union is a calculation, they will not hesitate to use it against me and, by extension, you."

"I assumed that was already the case," she reminded him carefully. "Our names are not without scandal."

"No. But we can still control the shape of it."

He stepped into the light now, the scar on his face catching the amber glow. "If it seems I have married for political favour or simply out of desperation, it will serve my enemies in the Lords. They will say I am not changing course, that I am only cloaking old ambition in a new narrative. Reform will be strangled before it ever finds breath."

She was watching him intently. "So... this marriage must appear genuine."

He nodded once. "As if we are what they never expected of us: two people who chose one another. Not out of duty but conviction. Affection, even."

The word hovered.

Affection.

It sounded foreign in this room. Especially in his mouth.

"And if it doesn't?" she asked softly. "If we do not convince them?"

"Then we both become figures of ridicule," he said. "You, the woman who bartered herself for a title. Me, the scarred relic, clawing back relevance through matrimony. We will be the tale whispered in every drawing room from Mayfair to Bath."

She looked away, to the fire. "You're very good at this."

"At what?"

"Turning everything into strategy."

He didn't deny it.

She lifted her eyes again. "What are you asking of me, exactly?"

His gaze held hers. "Let them believe it's real. Let them see something between us, some thread of connection they can't unpick."

Catharine stared at him, her heartbeat a slow, strange thud in her chest. She was no fool. She had known this would be a performance. She had planned for that. But somehow, she had not anticipated how close the performance would come to truth.

"Very well," she said at last. "We'll give them their illusion."

Alaric gave a slow nod. "It begins tomorrow. Let the maid who comes to stoke the fire in the morning see you in my bed. Let the staff see us take breakfast together. Let them see a wife who is not afraid of her husband's scar and a man who looks at his wife as if he sees only her."

"Can you do that?" she asked, walking over to the bed and sitting on the edge of it.

"I have led men into battle with less conviction than I plan to bring to this farce."

She almost smiled. Something in her chest loosened, but it did not ease. She was to be a wife who loved, but without the actual loving. It felt... painful.

***

Alaric moved towards her, taking a seat next to Catharine. They were side by side, close enough to feel the tension in the air between them but not touching.

Then there was a knock, soft but certain, at the chamber door.

"Enter," he said curtly.

The door creaked open, and a young maid stepped inside with a tray. She curtsied low, careful not to look too long at either of them.

"Tea, my lord. My lady."

She carried it to the side table and set it down gently, the porcelain clinking against silver. It contained two cups, a small pot, and a plate of sugared biscuits neither of them would touch.

"There's a draft coming in near the shutters," the girl added, glancing towards the tall windows. "Should I bring another log for the fire?"

"No," Alaric said. "That'll be all."

"Yes, my lord." Another curtsey. Her eyes flicked to the bed, probably without her meaning to. It was still neat, undisturbed save for Catharine's and his own rigid perch at its edge. Then the maid quickly glanced away. "Good night."

She withdrew. The door closed with a soft click. Silence settled again.

Catharine's voice, when it came, was low and deliberate, almost as if meant for herself. "And will you ask me to share your bed, for the sake of authenticity?"

She didn't look at him. She stared instead at the flames, as though the question was merely an observation about the weather or the hour. But he heard the tension behind it. He could understand that a woman, trapped in those circumstances, needed clarity. She needed terms.

He didn't move. "We will give them the truth of appearances. You will be seen in my chamber in the evenings. But I will not demand more."

That drew her eyes at last. Her gaze met his. A lesser woman might have blushed, stumbled over her modesty, or made some strained joke to dispel the moment. Catharine Fairbourne simply nodded once.

He was good at silence. After all, he had worn it like armour for years, but *this* one, with *this* woman, made it heavy in ways he hadn't anticipated.

Say something, he thought.

She turned slightly, enough for him to glimpse her eyes. There was something in them, something hesitant, as though she, too, felt the tension shimmering between them like a wire stretched too tightly. He reminded himself that she was nothing but a pawn in a game that was to benefit them both.

"There's something I would ask of you," she suddenly told him.

He straightened from where he sat at the edge of the bed, giving her his full attention. "Yes?"

Her composure had returned, but he could still sense the pulse beneath it, a steel mask over something more vulnerable.

"No more visits from Lady Miriam's women," she urged. "Not in this house."

Her tone left little room for argument. She wasn't pleading. Catharine Fairbourne did not plead. She was laying down a rule, plainly and without apology.

He inclined his head once. "Understood."

Her shoulders eased by a fraction. No smile followed. No softening of her beautiful facial features. But he saw something in her eyes. Relief, perhaps, disguised too well to name. Or maybe it was simply the barest hint of trust, carefully given.

She then gave a small nod, unreadable once more, and stood up.

"Good night, my lord," she said quietly.

He found his voice, rougher than he intended. "Good night, Catharine."

Her name felt unfamiliar in his mouth, but he liked the weight of it. She disappeared into the next room, the door shutting with a soft but final click. Alaric let out a breath he hadn't realised he'd been holding.

The chamber felt too large now, too quiet. He dragged a hand down his face, feeling his jaw tighten.

She was clever. But not only that, she was also beautiful, cold as marble, and just as composed. But he'd seen something flicker beneath the surface tonight, when she'd asked if he expected more, when she'd lingered at the door.

He had expected this arrangement to be inconvenient and politic. At worst, cold. But what he had not anticipated was this... awareness. Of her voice. Her scent. The fact that he'd wanted, just for a moment, to ask her to stay.

He poured himself a small measure of brandy and drank it in silence, staring into the fire.

This was a marriage of necessity, forged under the eye of society's scrutiny. A bargain and nothing more.

He would remember that.

He *had* to.

Chapter Nine

"You've hardly changed anything," Margaret said, stepping over the threshold with a rustle of pale muslin skirts and wide-eyed wonder. "It still feels like some old legend's home."

Catharine stood with her hands folded, watching as her younger sister crossed into the grand foyer of Ravensedge Hall with its arched ceilings shadowed and its tapestries faded with age but still rich with heraldry and stories long dead.

"I've been married less than a week," Catharine replied mildly. "I didn't intend to redecorate just yet."

Behind Margaret came Eliza, slower, more composed, her dark brows drawn slightly as she took in the hall. Her eyes, a deep hazel, swept over the stone floors, the iron sconces, the quiet hush that hung about the place like a secret. Eliza had always been the most observant of them, never quick to speak but difficult to fool.

Margaret turned to Catharine and clasped her gloved hands. "You look so well," she said with honest affection. "Marriage suits you."

Catharine gave her a small nod. "Thank you."

Eliza didn't echo the sentiment. Instead, she wandered to the foot of the great staircase, where a threadbare crimson runner led into the deeper halls of the estate. Her fingers brushed one of the carved banisters, the faintest frown tugging at her lips.

"The wedding was quite... unorthodox," Eliza said at last. Her voice was even, but the words held weight. "It happened so quickly. I'm sure people are still talking."

"They are," Catharine said calmly. "They will for some time, no doubt."

Margaret glanced between them, her smile faltering as she sensed the subtle tension.

"You could have written to me about it," Eliza said, turning back towards her. "You didn't even let me know until the morning of the ceremony that you would be marrying a different man. You sent a single letter with no explanation."

Catharine's eyes met hers. "There wasn't time for more."

"That's not an answer."

"No," she said softly. "It isn't."

Eliza's expression flickered, and there was something sharp behind her gaze. Concern or accusation, Catharine couldn't quite tell. Perhaps both. But Eliza, for all her tact, had never mastered the art of silence when it mattered most.

"You must admit," Eliza went on, stepping closer, "it seems rather unlike you. To marry so suddenly. And... *him.*"

"Lord Ravensedge," Catharine corrected with a cool lift of her chin.

Eliza folded her arms. "Yes. The marquess, whose face is half scar and half myth, depending on whom you ask."

"Eliza," Margaret whispered, a touch scandalised.

"I'm only repeating what's already been said," Eliza replied, unapologetic. "It's not gossip if it's general knowledge."

Catharine exhaled through her nose, measured and controlled. "If you came here expecting scandal, I'm afraid you'll be disappointed."

"I came here to understand why you did it," Eliza said.

And that, Catharine thought, was the trouble. No one, not even her sisters, could understand. Because it hadn't been a surrender to romance or a desperate lunge towards security. It had been a decision, precise and cold and necessary. And in the echo of that silence between them, she felt again the weight of what she'd agreed to, the things she'd given up for the sake of duty and name.

"I made a choice," she said finally. "And I don't intend to explain myself further."

Margaret stepped in quickly, looping an arm through Catharine's. "She looks well, doesn't she?" she said again with forced brightness. "And Ravensedge is quite... grand. Isn't it?"

Eliza said nothing. But her eyes, those clever hazel eyes, continued to search the walls, stone and tapestry alike, for whatever truth Catharine wasn't saying.

They had moved to the small salon by then, the one Catharine had ordered opened and aired just for this visit. It caught the late afternoon light through the long windows, glinting against porcelain figures and a scattering of books Catharine had already begun to inspect.

Catharine stood by the window, her fingers curled lightly around the back of a chair. She could feel Eliza's gaze again, less piercing now and more hesitant.

"I just want you to be happy," Eliza said quietly.

The gentleness in her voice startled Catharine more than any accusation might have. She turned her head slowly. Eliza no longer looked like the woman who stalked drawing rooms in London with a raised eyebrow and a cutting quip. Her arms were folded, but her stance had softened, her mouth turned down in the smallest of frowns.

"I don't need to be happy," she said, too quickly.

Eliza's brow furrowed momentarily.

"I need to be useful," Catharine added, quieter now. "I need to secure what's left of our family's dignity. I need to give Margaret a future unmarred by our name becoming a subject of pity."

"But that isn't—"

"Eliza." Catharine met her gaze, steady despite the ache behind it. "Don't make this harder than it is."

Eliza's jaw tensed, and for a breath, she looked like she might argue. But then she sighed and crossed the room in a few quick steps. Her hands closed over Catharine's, her cold fingers wrapped in warm ones.

"I'm not here to fight you," she said. "I'm here because I missed you. And because I couldn't make sense of any of this without seeing your face."

Catharine swallowed. "And what do you see?"

Her sister gave a faint smile. "I see someone who looks exhausted. And proud. And..."—she hesitated, her thumb brushing Catharine's knuckles—"someone who's trying not to drown."

Catharine looked down, the words hitting closer than she wanted to admit. But she didn't have much time to linger on her thoughts and feelings because of the soft scrape of the door and a flurry of brisk steps in the corridor, which drew all of their attention. Moments later, the door opened, and in swept Lady Isadora Vale, as vibrant and self-assured as ever, her walking cloak still draped elegantly over one shoulder.

"Well, I see the new Lady Ravensedge keeps fine company," she declared, her voice rich and unapologetic.

"Eliza. Margaret," Catharine said, turning with a flicker of surprise that quickly smoothed into composure. "You remember Lady Isadora, my husband's cousin."

"Of course," Eliza said, rising. "I remember you from Lady Willoughby's ball a few years ago, when you played the piano beautifully. You haven't changed a bit."

"Oh, I should hope I have," Lady Isadora replied with a wink, unfastening her cloak and handing it off to a maid who had appeared at her elbow. "Improvement is the whole point of widowhood, darling. Less husband, more fun."

Margaret stifled a delighted giggle behind her hand, and even Eliza's lips twitched.

Catharine gestured towards the settee. "Please, join us."

Isadora sank into the cushions with the grace of someone born to dominate a room. Her eyes sparkled. "So. You've probably all come to inspect the mysterious union. And you found my cousin still brooding, still impossible, and still with no idea how to make polite conversation."

Eliza laughed. It was an actual laugh, not a dry huff or a tight-lipped smirk. "That sounds about right."

"Oh, he's a menace," Lady Isadora said, waving a hand. "He was practically raised by wolves and hasn't improved much with age. But..." She leaned in, her tone more sincere now. "He is loyal. Utterly. Once he gives a damn about someone, he will burn down the world before letting harm come to them."

Catharine felt the stillness of her sisters beside her. Even Margaret looked serious now.

"I'm not saying he's easy," Lady Isadora went on, smoothing the fabric of her skirts. "But if he's chosen you, Catharine, then

I have no doubt he'll stand by you. Whether you want him to or not."

Catharine's throat felt tight again, but she managed a small nod.

"Well," Margaret said brightly, "I suppose if Lady Isadora approves, then we can give him a little more credit."

Lady Isadora arched a playful brow. "Oh, don't go too far. He's still utterly hopeless at dancing and has the bedside manner of a wet boot. But he's ours."

That earned more laughter, real laughter this time. Catharine found herself exhaling and some of the heaviness in her chest lifting. She was still balancing on the edge of something she couldn't quite name, but for the first time in a few days, the weight of it all didn't feel entirely unbearable.

The conversation turned to lighter matters: travel, gowns, and the unflattering fashions of the Duchess of Pembroke, and for a while, it felt almost ordinary. As if this had always been her home, as if, perhaps, it still could be.

After her sisters departed with hugs and promises to write, the echo of their carriage wheels faded into the afternoon wind. The house, once again, fell into its usual silence. Catharine stood in the entrance hall for a moment longer than necessary, her eyes lingering on the door as if she might summon them back just by wishing it. But wishes, she knew, were useless things.

She turned and ascended the stairs with deliberate care. Her steps led her instinctively down the guest corridor, which was an old habit from childhood, where she would often check the rooms after visitors left, as if tidying up their presence might help steady her own mind. It was then she heard it: a low, rhythmic tapping, like knuckles on wood.

Tap. Tap.

The sound came from the far end of the corridor. She followed it, frowning, until she reached the small guest room near the corner turret. The wind had picked up outside, pushing against the old stone walls. One of the windows rattled in protest, the pane shivering in its frame.

She stepped closer and saw that the latch had come loose, the metal catch just out of reach from where she stood. The chill had already crept into the room, lifting the curtains slightly with each gust. Catharine stretched up, trying to hook the latch, but the sill was too high.

She tried again, this time standing on tiptoe, bracing her hand against the wall for balance. A gust hit the pane just then, harder than the rest. The window groaned, and she stumbled back a step, her skirts catching on the edge of a low chest. She let out a sharp breath and cursed softly under it.

She hated needing help. Still, the window wouldn't close by itself. She figured she would send for a footman, perhaps, but as she did, a voice startled her from behind.

"You'll catch a chill doing that."

She stiffened, turning halfway before she felt him step in close... too close.

Alaric's presence filled the small space like a tidal wave. One hand braced the wall above her shoulder, and the other reached around her, brushing hers as he took hold of the latch. His chest pressed lightly against her back, his breath warm against the shell of her ear.

She didn't move. She couldn't.

The air between them shifted, thick and brittle. The smell of leather and cedar clung to him. It was earthy, sharp, unmistakably *his*. Her spine locked rigidly, though her heart had taken up a furious rhythm she couldn't quite tame.

The latch gave way with a final *click*.

Still, he didn't step back.

Catharine swallowed. Her gaze flicked to the window, then the floor, then anywhere else that might keep her from turning her head and seeing how close his mouth was to her temple. But she felt it, the way his breath slowed, how his body didn't retreat but lingered, as if considering something.

She felt his fingers slide lower, tracing the slope of her neck as he dropped his arm. The touch was brief. It wasn't accidental.

A shiver rose despite the warmth now flooding her veins.

He exhaled, a low sound barely louder than the wind beyond the pane.

"I'll have the window replaced," he murmured near her ear, his voice almost too deep, too quiet to trust. "It's old."

Then, without another sound, he stepped away. The air cooled again at once.

She turned, but he was already at the doorway, and a moment later, he was gone. Catharine stayed where she stood, the rattle of the wind now silent behind the closed window. Her neck still tingled where his fingers had touched it.

She pressed a hand to her chest and exhaled.

Whatever this marriage was becoming, it was far more dangerous to her peace of mind than she had planned.

Chapter Ten

"The floor recognises the Right Honourable Lord Bramley," intoned the Lord Chancellor from the woolsack, his voice echoing beneath the lofty hammer-beam ceiling of the chamber.

Alaric shifted in his seat near the crossbenches, the crimson leather warm beneath his gloved palms. His gaze swept the vaulted expanse of the House of Lords: the dark oak panelling, the tall stained-glass windows filtering pale daylight, and the rows of peers draped in their scarlet robes or navy frock coats, their white cravats stark against flushed or jowled faces.

The chamber was full. More than full, in fact. It was brimming with tension. Alaric felt it in the way men turned their heads subtly, casting sidelong glances in his direction, in the murmured rustle of silk cuffs and notes being passed from page boys to ministers. His presence, and more importantly, his sudden marriage, had not gone unnoticed.

Lord Bramley, a gaunt man with a haughty air and a nasal delivery, rose with a sheaf of papers in hand. "This proposed treaty with the North Sea League threatens to destabilise the grain tariffs which have safeguarded British landowners for decades. I ask—no, I insist—that we consider the implications for our own farmers before we open our ports in such reckless fashion."

Predictable.

Alaric leaned back, letting the speech roll over him. He had already read the treaty twice and scribbled more annotations in its margins than his secretaries appreciated. It was, in truth, sound. A delicate but necessary shift in foreign alignment. But Bramley was not interested in diplomacy, only in preserving old leverage and undermining any man who challenged the status quo.

"Does the Marquess of Ravensedge have a comment?" came the Lord Chancellor again.

Alaric rose.

"The agricultural protections in question," he commenced, well prepared for the topic in question, "will remain intact for our domestic suppliers. The language in Article Six explicitly limits competition to seasonal goods and maritime commerce. What Lord Bramley fails to mention, whether by ignorance or design, is that the agreement ensures reciprocal protection for our own exports, particularly cotton and steel."

Murmurs fluttered through the chamber.

Bramley's face had reddened. "Are we to believe you, Lord Ravensedge," he sneered, "a man who barely set foot in Parliament for the better part of five years until you found yourself in need of a political resurrection?"

The jibe was cheap and even more so, the intent obvious. Alaric's smile, though, was slow and calculated.

"I prefer to let the quality of my proposals speak louder than the quantity of my appearances. But if Lord Bramley would like to discuss absences, perhaps we ought to consult the records from last September's votes, when he was otherwise occupied with his... *business* in Brighton."

Business was, of course, a euphemism for mistress, and everyone knew it, although no one dared agree with it.

At that moment, Lord Blackmoor rose with the elegance of a man who had never fought for anything but his own comfort. His dark frock coat was immaculate, his hair perfectly pomaded.

"While the marquess makes a good point," Blackmoor began, folding his hands behind his back, "some of us remain concerned with matters closer to home. The character of a statesman, for example. His personal conduct. His moral judgement. These things, I daresay, are not merely private matters. They are the bedrock of public trust."

The words dropped with slow, deliberate weight. There was no question who they were meant for, yet again.

Blackmoor continued in a pleasant tone of voice. "It would be a shame if hastily formed alliances were to cast doubt upon a man's motivations in this chamber."

Alaric felt the stir around him, the way curiosity tilted like a weathervane towards scandal. Some peers leaned in. Others looked away, pretending not to enjoy the spectacle.

Before he himself could rise, another voice spoke.

"I think we all might benefit," said Lord Huckleby mildly, "from returning to the topic at hand, which was military reform. Not matrimony. Not moral parables. The men in uniform who serve this country, after all, require more than insinuations and anecdotes."

Huckleby was old, clever, and utterly unflappable. His white brows arched gently over shrewd eyes. His intervention was pointed. It was, in fact, less a defence of Alaric and more a reminder that personal slander disguised as policy debate was a waste of the Parliament's time. The chamber quieted.

Alaric gave a single, curt nod of acknowledgment. *Thank you,* it meant. Nothing more.

The vote proceeded. Alaric raised his hand with mechanical precision, his eyes scanning the dark wood-panelled chamber as the tally was called. The motion carried, albeit narrowly. Applause was muted, the outcome secondary to the unsaid.

No direct accusations had surfaced. At least, not today.

But the whispers that bloomed in the wake of Blackmoor's performance were pointed enough. He caught them as he passed: clipped phrases, murmured conjectures exchanged behind gloves and tilted canes.

"... Fairbourne girl, wasn't she passed over once already...?"

"... convenient timing, don't you think...?"

"... desperate to restore his reputation... clever match, if cold..."

They hadn't spoken his name. But they had spoken *hers,* and that was worse.

Alaric descended the stone steps outside the chamber, the great doors of Westminster Hall yawning open before him, swallowing up light. The weight returned, that ever-familiar pressure beneath his ribs. It had lived in him for years now, tucked beneath the scars and layered behind every calculation.

He had thought marriage might shift it. Not alleviate it, not wholly, but at least tilt the shape of the burden. Now he wasn't sure if what he'd done hadn't actually worsened his position.

Those were the thoughts swirling inside his mind as he rode through the city as twilight gathered over rooftops like a silken net. His greatcoat flared behind him as he took the turning towards Mayfair, muscle memory guiding the reins more than intent. The streets narrowed the closer he drew to Lady Miriam's townhouse. Pale gaslight flickered in the windows, catching on the lace curtain that had once signalled her availability. The door was painted a modest green, which almost made it respectably welcoming.

He reined in just short of it. No one came out to greet him or welcome him. That was part of the arrangement: Lady Miriam's establishment required neither introductions nor explanations. For years, it had been his retreat from the constraints of rank, duty, and decency. When he'd returned from Spain half-alive and fully broken, Lady Miriam hadn't flinched at the sight of the scar that tore from temple to jaw. She'd only asked what he preferred to drink and then what he preferred in a woman.

Tonight, though, he didn't dismount. The horse shifted beneath him, snorting softly. Alaric loosened his grip on the reins, but he didn't move to tie them.

He could go inside. He could forget last week. But he could never forget Catharine's face, not even for a single moment.

Damn it.

Alaric swore under his breath, a low rasp of sound that startled his mount. He gripped the reins harder and turned the horse without another glance at the townhouse.

He would not go inside. Not tonight, or any other night, for that matter.

The ride back to Ravensedge was long and silent, the night wind cruel against his face. He welcomed the sting. It reminded him that he was still alive, and that choices, however small or seemingly insignificant, still mattered.

So did sleep, but that night, it failed to grace him with its blissful presence. Alaric lay flat on his back with one arm draped across his eyes and the other fisted in the sheets. The fire had long since burned low, but heat coiled in his gut like an ember that refused to die.

He had doused the candles himself, stalked the room like a man half-hunted, then poured a second and then also a third glass of brandy, and still, nothing quieted the noise in his head. His body, just like his mind, simply refused to settle. His jaw ached from clenching. Every muscle was wound tight, every breath shallow. He shifted beneath the covers, cursed, kicked them off, then yanked them back again with a hiss of frustration.

He sat up on the edge of the bed, raking his fingers through his hair.

"It makes no sense," he murmured to himself. "She isn't even my type."

That much was true. She was too cold, too stubborn, too damn calculating, all polish and poise, with eyes like winger glass.

And yet... the memory of her scent haunted him. The feel of their fingers brushing against each other tantalised him. It should have meant nothing. He'd held dying men in his arms. Heck, he'd kissed women whose names he never asked. That was why this absurd flicker of something he refused to identify should not linger.

He turned onto his side. Then onto his back again.

The truth, unwelcome and undeniable, pressed hard against his chest: he'd begun to wonder what she might sound like if she ever stopped being polite. He wondered what would happen if her voice dropped, if her careful posture gave way, if she ever said his name not with obligation but with want.

He groaned low in his throat, dragging a hand over his face.

This wasn't the plan. She was meant to be useful, nothing else. She was supposed to be a balm to his reputation, a political alliance, a woman with ambition enough to overlook his scars, his name, his past. He had chosen her *precisely* because he did not want her. And now he could not stop thinking about her.

He was not in love. He did not even like her, if he was honest with himself. But desire was a different matter. It was a sensation much darker and much more dangerous. It needed no permission, no affection. It simply *was*.

He ran a hand down his bare arm, over the long scar on his shoulder. The firelight caught the edge of it, making it appear even more jagged. He had thought himself long past the foolishness of wanting what he could not have. But apparently not.

Eventually, near dawn, sleep found him. It was a restless, shallow thing, filled with half-dreams and the scent of jasmine.

Chapter Eleven

"Lady Ravensedge?"

Catharine turned, only to see a footman standing at the far end of the corridor.

"Yes?" she replied.

He bowed. "I believe the brooch you asked after was found. A maid thought she saw it atop the marble table by the west bathing chamber."

"Thank you."

She offered the barest nod and dismissed him with a glance. As he disappeared down the hall, she adjusted her shawl and continued in the direction of the bathing rooms.

The corridor was dim and quiet at this hour, the house asleep but not silent. She heard the wind outside, as well as the faint tick of the longcase clock downstairs. She walked with purpose, but her thoughts were scattered—something she despised.

The brooch was not valuable, at least not in the way society measured such things. But it had belonged to her mother, a modest silver crescent inlaid with tiny seed pearls. It was the only piece Catharine had worn during her first engagement, which she also considered her first humiliation.

Catharine reached the west wing and slowed. The air was cooler here, touched by the drafts that slid through old stone. The bathing chambers were tucked near the end of the corridor, and so she sensibly assumed that they would be empty.

It was near midnight. Servants had long since retired. Even if they did have guests, no one would be foolish enough to brave the chill for a bath at this hour.

So when she opened the door, she did not expect to find *him*.

Lord Ravensedge stood shirtless with his back to her, the scarred plane of his shoulders slick with water and firelight. He had just stepped from the bath. He had a towel hanging low on his hips. He did not turn, but she saw the way his spine stiffened at the sound of the door.

Her throat closed before she could speak. Her body immediately went still.

She should have left. She meant to, she *truly* did.

But something pinned her there. It was not a scandal, though a scandal surely hovered close under these circumstances, but the sheer startling presence of him. She had seen him in drawing rooms, at dinners, stiff with civility and discomfort in equal measure. But this... this was not the man she had agreed to marry. This man was *real*.

He turned slowly, as if he had all the time in the world.

"Lady Ravensedge," he said in a voice that made her insides tighten into a knot. "Have you lost your way in this big house?"

She forced her eyes to meet his and nothing lower. "I was told my brooch was here."

He said nothing. A droplet of water traced down his neck.

"I'll retrieve it and go," she added, swallowing heavily. But her steps faltered as she moved forward because he didn't look away. His gaze held hers like a challenge.

The brooch sat on the edge of the marble table, exactly where the maid had said. She picked it up, clasped it with a practiced hand, and turned to leave.

But then he spoke again. "Tell me something, Lady Ravensedge. Do you always keep your armour on, even when no one's watching?"

She stopped, her hand tightening around the brooch. Her back was to him. It was safer that way.

"You mistake self-possession for armour, my lord."

"Do I?"

She didn't say anything to that. Neither did she move, as steam pressed damp against her skin. Her lungs refused to expand properly.

Then she heard him move. She heard that quiet slap of his wet, bare feet against the tiled floor. His pace was unhurried, and that was the maddening part. He was controlled, measured. He was coming closer and closer. She felt it not just in the sound but also in the air shifting behind her, in the space shrinking between them.

Still, she refused to turn. Her pulse pounded furiously, traitorously, in her throat. Her body knew what it wanted. Her mind recoiled.

"Are you too shy," he drawled softly, "or too afraid to gaze upon your husband?"

The word landed with a curious weight. *Husband.* In their case, it meant a man chosen for reasons that had nothing to do with how he made her skin tighten and her stomach clench. Yet something had happened.

She turned slowly, lifting her chin as their eyes met.

"Neither."

The corners of his mouth tugged, not quite a smile but something darker, as if he knew something she herself did not. Then he stepped closer. She didn't move, not out of bravery, but because her legs wouldn't obey her. He stopped only when there was no space left. Her back was nearly against the door. She was trapped, and yet she didn't feel like prey.

Their eyes locked. She told herself not to look lower. She failed miserably. His chest rose and fell, water still clinging to his skin. A small droplet slid down from his collarbone, caught the edge of an old scar, and vanished.

His hand lifted. She flinched when he touched her. Surprisingly, his touch was featherlight. She had no idea why she expected him to be rough. He reached for a loose curl that had escaped her braid, caught it between his fingers, and let it slide through as if memorising the weight of it.

Then, slowly, his hand dropped to her jaw. His thumb brushed the edge of her chin. She hated how her breath hitched, how all he needed to do was look at her face, and every single thought she had was revealed to him.

"I was thinking about you all night," he murmured in a deep and husky voice that made her skin erupt in gooseflesh.

Catharine couldn't look away. Her throat worked around the answer she wouldn't say. *So was I.*

She didn't know how to survive this. She didn't know what it meant. Was it desire? Proximity? Frustration? Was she merely the nearest body to a man worn thin by solitude and scandal?

He didn't leer. He didn't push. He just looked at her like a man starving but not yet reaching for the table.

Then his mouth descended on hers, and she did nothing to stop him. She kissed him back because something inside her snapped free. The mask, the calculation, the cold strategy all shattered the moment his lips found hers.

It was a wild, hungry kiss, not the kiss of a careful man or a patient, calculating woman. It was a kiss that consumed.

Her fingers found his shoulders, then gripped him hard. His body was heat and strength and something almost unbearable, all in one. She didn't remember when her eyes closed, only that the world dropped away. There was only the press of his mouth, the slide of his hand at her waist, the unrelenting fire that spread through her like fever.

Desire for him was burning her up alive, and she didn't know if this was weakness or simply the truth. She only knew that she had never kissed anyone like this, and that no one had ever kissed *her* like she mattered.

But then, just as suddenly as he had kissed her, he pulled away. The loss of him made her sway before she caught herself. His breath was still harsh against her cheek, and it was the only sound between them save for the steady drip of water onto the tile. His hand lingered at her jaw for a moment longer. Then it, too, fell away.

"If you are not certain," he said in a low and dark tone of voice, "that you want to be mine, right now, right here... then go."

The words were a challenge. They were also a warning. And finally, they were a raw kind of honesty she hadn't expected from him.

She didn't move at first. Because... what was it that he truly demanded of her? Certainty?

If that was what he required of her, she could not give it. Not because she didn't want him, but exactly because the opposite was true. She wanted him so much that it utterly terrified her.

Wanting had betrayed her before. It had made her a fool in silk slippers, waiting for a man who never came. It had dragged her name through every drawing room in town. It had left her sister whispering apologies for things that weren't her fault.

And now, here, in this heated room with steam curling around her like smoke and her body still aching from the taste of his mouth, she was dangerously close to wanting again.

Reason surfaced through the haze of confusion. She turned around and, without speaking, headed towards the door. She didn't even glance back. She pulled the door open and walked out with each step, feeling as if she had broken something with her own hands.

Once out in the corridor, cool air slapped her cheeks, forcing more common sense into her thoughts. Now with a slightly clearer head, she walked briskly back towards her chamber, hoping to make it before her knees weakened.

There, alone in the dim silence, Catharine let herself exhale.

It was wrong. Everything about him was completely and utterly consuming. He was dangerous, not in the way of scoundrels or libertines but in the way a wildfire is dangerous, unpredictable, and devouring everything in its path. She had lived her life by calculation, by the mastery of feeling, by the belief that composure was safety.

To give in to *him* would be her undoing. And she would be damned if she allowed that to happen. Everything depended on her staying in control.

She pressed the brooch against her palm until the sharp edge bit into her skin, almost as a reminder of who she was, who she could never be again, of what she had built, and finally of what it had cost her.

Let the fire burn, she thought to herself. *I will not step into it.*

Chapter Twelve

"You look like hell, Ravensedge."

Alaric didn't look up from the papers spread across his desk. "Good morning to you, too, Gainsworth."

Lord Dorian Gainsworth strode into the study without waiting to be invited, as he always did. He was dressed in his usual fashion, showcasing elegance without being ostentatious, with an expression that suggested mild amusement at the rest of the world's ineptitude at the same skill.

He dropped into the chair opposite Alaric with the ease of a man who had known him too long and been given too few reasons to leave.

"I was up reading your speech from last session," Dorian said, stretching his legs out. "You were right, by the way. The shipping bill's a disaster. Parliament will choke on it, mark my words."

"They already are," Alaric replied, finally lifting his gaze. "They just haven't figured out who to blame."

Dorian gave him a meaningful look. "They'll find a way. And I expect you'll be conveniently at hand."

Alaric's mouth twisted, not quite a smile but still a sign of amused agreement.

They settled into a rhythm quickly. Long years of friendship had carved out a space for it, even now. The conversation turned to the usual: grain tariffs, naval spending, the quiet tug-of-war over East India Company contracts. Dorian's mind was sharp and his instincts shrewd, as always. He was one of the few men left in London who still spoke to Alaric without false deference or veiled disdain. But eventually, as well as inevitably, the conversation turned.

"So," Dorian said, casually folding one ankle over his knee. "It would appear that there has been a significant change in your marital status as of late."

Alaric didn't blink. "Apparently so."

"Apparently?" Dorian raised both brows. "You make it sound as if you stumbled into a marriage over brandy and you were too polite to protest."

Alaric leaned back in his chair, with his fingers steepled. "The arrangement is... practical."

Complicated was the first thing that popped to mind, but that would require more explanation of him, and Alaric was in no mood for lengthy elaborations on his marital status.

"Practical," Dorian repeated dryly. "She's Fairbourne's daughter. She was a society darling not long ago. Jilted, if I remember right, which makes her nearly as scandalous as you."

Twice. But again, Alaric kept that to himself.

"We suit each other," he said instead.

"That," Dorian said with a small laugh, "is the most romantic thing I've ever heard."

Alaric didn't respond. His gaze shifted to the window, where pale morning light was just beginning to touch the edge of the stone sill.

Dorian tilted his head. "You know I don't care if you married her out of convenience, desperation, or boredom. I just want to know if it's going to work for you."

"It will," Alaric said.

His tone of voice was flat and utterly unconvincing.

Dorian caught his friend's hesitation. He always did. "You're not the sort to take a wife just to please the papers or Parliament."

"I'm the sort who understands leverage," Alaric replied. "She has a name, reputation, and the kind of resilience that doesn't require fainting couches."

"Sounds like admiration."

"It's mere observation."

Before Dorian could say anything to that, the door to Alaric's study swung open with the brisk decisiveness of someone who wasn't used to knocking.

Isadora stepped into the study with a smile, but as soon as her eyes fell on Lord Gainsworth, her composure became that of a general entering hostile territory.

"Alaric, I came to ask you if you've had breakfast yet," she told him. "I didn't realise you were... entertaining."

Dorian rose leisurely from his chair, his face graced with the faintest smirk tugging at his mouth. "Ah, Lady Izza. How charming to see you again."

"It's Lady *Isadora*," she corrected him. "Izza is just for friends, which we, Lord Gainsworth, are not."

"My apologies," he said, with a mock half-bow with his hand pressed to his chest. "I see you are still fond of storming into rooms uninvited."

"And you," she said, returning his smile with an expression that could curdle wine, "still haven't learned the difference between wit and noise."

The air in the study turned taut. Alaric leaned back in his chair, watching them with the detachment of a man observing a fencing match he had no intention of interrupting.

"I assumed you would be finished with his business by now," Isadora said, turning slightly towards Alaric, though her eyes did not leave Gainsworth. "Clearly, I was mistaken."

"Politics is rarely swift," Dorian replied.

She gave a crisp nod. "And yet some men take longer to say very little."

Dorian laughed, seeming infuriatingly amused. "You wound me, my lady."

"You'll recover," she said sweetly.

He took a step towards her, not threatening but with the ease of someone perfectly at home in every room. "Your disdain is noted. Though I admit I'm flattered... it suggests you think me worth the effort."

"Hardly." She folded her gloves slowly. "I simply have no patience for men who flatter themselves with empty charm and forgettable arguments."

Dorian's smile deepened. "Admit it. You've been thinking about me."

She rolled her eyes. "I was thinking about breakfast. Now I've lost my appetite."

Alaric said nothing. He wouldn't have interrupted if the roof had caught fire. There was something almost mesmerising about the way they moved around each other, all those barbs polished to brilliance, every word a strike or parry.

That was when Isadora turned on her heel. Her skirt sliced through the air like a blade. "Alaric, come find me in the garden when your guest has finished performing."

Alaric expected a slammed door, but instead, what he heard was a pointed click.

Dorian exhaled loudly, clearly enjoying himself. "She's delightful."

Alaric lifted a brow. "You goad her deliberately."

"She rises beautifully to it."

"You keep poking, and she'll draw blood."

Dorian grinned. "That's what makes it interesting."

Alaric shook his head, reaching for the stack of correspondence on his desk and handing the top letter to Dorian, ending the subject. A while later, Dorian stood up.

"I should go," he informed his friend, keeping two letters in his hand. "I'll keep these, just in case. I want to go over the shipping bill again."

"By all means." Alaric nodded.

Dorian paused by the door, one hand resting lightly on the handle. "You know," he added, "your cousin would make a fascinating chess opponent. If she ever let anyone close enough to play, that is."

Alaric glanced up, just once. "She would win. And she wouldn't let you forget it."

Dorian's smile curved slightly. "Precisely why I'm tempted."

Then he tipped his head and took his leave. Alaric exhaled. The room was suddenly quieter, though not calmer. He stood, walked to the window, and braced one hand on the sill. London's pale light filtered through the gauze curtains. Somewhere below, a cart rattled down the street.

He should have felt more focused. He didn't. A knock on the door came as a welcome distraction.

He turned, half-expecting the butler. "Yes?"

The door opened just enough to admit a sliver of dark blue skirts and a familiar posture. It was Isadora again.

He lifted a brow. "You're knocking this time?"

It didn't escape his attention that she glanced across his study to assure herself that he was alone. She stepped inside with less fire this time, and her composure returned to its usual elegance.

"I already interrupted you once today." She smiled playfully. "Twice would be considered utterly rude of me."

He arched a brow. "Couldn't bear to leave without a second round?"

"I cannot possibly know what you mean, dear cousin," she replied sweetly. But one look in his direction assured her that they both knew the reference. She cleared her throat and continued. "I believe I've made my point."

He couldn't resist asking. "How do you know Dorian?"

There it was: the smallest of pauses. There was a flicker of something veiled and secretive behind her eyes. It vanished almost immediately, replaced with polite indifference.

"Lord Gainsworth and I have crossed paths before," she said. "At Lady Brixton's house party last summer, I believe. And again during Lord Willoughby's ball."

"That's all?"

She lifted one shoulder in a careless shrug. "I don't know what you mean by *all*. We danced at a ball. We realised that we... *tolerate* each other. He finds me difficult. I find him ridiculous."

He found that difficult to believe. "You were nearly spitting fire ten minutes ago."

"That *is* me being tolerant." He snorted, but he didn't get a chance for any retort because she quickly added, changing the topic, "There is a gathering at the Duchess of Merriton's townhouse three nights from now."

"And?" he inquired indifferently.

"And you're expected to attend," she replied, arching one brow. "With your wife."

He gave a low exhale, which was not quite a sigh and even further away from relief. "A room full of aristocrats waiting to dissect my face and her reputation... charming."

"It will be worse if you don't show," Isadora said crisply. "Your enemies will call it weakness. Hers will call it shame."

He had to admit that she had a point. Public appearances had always mattered, but now, with his sudden marriage and alliances shifting like sand underfoot, every nod, every glance, every absence carried weight. Their marriage was more than personal; it was political theatre. And the audience was hungry.

"Fine," Alaric acquiesced. "We'll go."

"Try to wear something without blood on it," she teased. "And try not to scowl, if only just for the evening."

He gave her a flat look. "Anything else?"

She turned then but paused again at the threshold, her fingers trailing the edge of the doorframe.

"Yes. Catharine's birthday is the day after tomorrow," she said lightly, almost as if it had just occurred to her. "I doubt she'll mention it. She doesn't care for celebrations."

His brows knitted. "Then why tell me?"

"Because she won't," Isadora replied simply. "And because I suspect you're clever enough to do something with the knowledge."

She didn't wait for a response, and the door closed gently behind her.

Catharine's birthday.

He hadn't known. Of course, she wouldn't tell him. A woman like that would never admit to desiring softness, not even for a single day out of the year. Because to be celebrated required being seen, and to be seen required risk. He didn't know much about his wife, but he did know one thing: She would risk nothing she couldn't control.

That was why he wasn't surprised to hear the soft sound of the adjoining door opening that night. He watched as Catharine stepped through without a single word. Silently, she sipped beneath the covers beside him.

Her body was cool against the warmth he had built, and the sheets shifted slightly between them as she settled. She faced away, her breathing even and composed. Her every movement was controlled, as if she had rehearsed it.

He lay completely still, staring at the canopy overhead. The faint scent of rosewater clung to her skin, ghosting between them like an unanswered question. Momentarily, a maid knocked and then, after being called forth, entered. She smiled as she checked the hearth and drew the curtains closed. She placed a carafe on the bedside table and murmured a good night. Then the door shut softly behind her.

And as soon as the latch clicked into place, Catharine rose, still without a word. She moved efficiently without any rush but with the unmistakable manner of a woman who had no interest in remaining where she was not fully at ease. She crossed the room, disappeared back through the adjoining door, and was gone.

Alaric exhaled slowly, a long breath through his nose. The pillow beside him held the faint indent of her shape. The sheet was still warm where she had lain. He turned on his side and closed his eyes, but sleep did not come. He could still feel the warmth she'd left behind.

And the chill she took with her when she left.

Chapter Thirteen

When sleep finally came, it did not come gently.

It was restless and fevered, filled with fragments that refused to cohere. She was haunted by shadows of hands that had never truly touched her. She felt heat where none should be. And she could sense the unmistakable scent of cedar and clean soap that belonged only to *him*.

In the dream, she wasn't guarded. She wasn't calculating. She was *his*.

His mouth had found hers without warning or permission. And just like before, she hadn't stopped him. Instead, she had reached for him, gasping into the kiss like a woman who had gone too long without air. His hands had cupped her face, slid down her neck, caught at the thin shift that clung to her skin. His mouth had moved along her jaw, across the pulse at her throat, and every rule she had ever lived by, every mask she had ever worn, shattered in an instant.

She stirred in the sheets.

A soft sound escaped her lips. "Alaric..."

The name broke into the darkness, no louder than a whisper, but it pierced the quiet like a struck chord. She shifted again, her legs tangling in the linen as the heat of the dream clung to her like sweat. Her hands curled into the pillow as if seeking the weight of him, yearning for the anchor of his body against hers.

When she opened her eyes, she saw him standing in the doorway between their chambers. He had been watching her. His expression revealed nothing, but his eyes... she saw a storm inside of them.

"You called out my name," he murmured, looking at her with that same unbearable stillness, like a man weighing what could be taken without permission and what might be given if asked for in the right manner.

Heat rushed to her cheeks, but she didn't look away. Her hands gripped the coverlet, her fingers twisting in the linen. She opened her mouth to deny it, but the lie withered on her tongue.

His gaze drifted over her. He noticed how her nightgown came down her shoulder. He took a step closer to her.

"Was I in your dream, Catharine?" he asked, calm but dangerous, like flint struck just before a flame. "Or did you say my name because you wanted me to come?"

He reached the foot of the bed, then he stopped. "Tell me of the fire that consumes you."

Her fingers trembled slightly at the coverlet, shaking her head. "I'll be burned…"

His fingers curled around the edges of the coverlet, pulling it off of her slowly. She allowed him. His hand slid to her thigh, pausing just above the knee where the silk of her nightgown had ridden up.

"Then let me show you that not all heat harms…"

He kissed her like he had something to prove, but not to her… to himself, perhaps, or to whatever part of him still doubted he could touch something without breaking it.

Catharine matched him at first, kiss for kiss, hunger for hunger. But it wasn't just desire that surged between them. It was *need*, knotted tight with uncertainty. Every breath they took was shared. Every movement was cautious and charged, as if neither of them could quite believe that this moment was real but was merely a dream they were sharing.

When he pulled away, she couldn't even begin to comprehend what he had in mind. His eyes burned with passion as he lowered himself to his knees, gently gripping the hem of her delicate nightgown with his fingers. She looked down at him, swallowing heavily.

Surely, he doesn't mean to—

But her thoughts were silenced by the act of his hand gently settling her thigh on his shoulder and lifting her nightgown up until there was nothing covering her.

"Alaric." She whispered his name again as excitement overpowered the bashfulness in her voice.

He didn't say anything. He couldn't, for his lips were already on her skin, searing into it. He lifted his head as his eyes locked with hers, and the sight stole her breath away. She could see his entire tongue spread out, gently licking her most sensitive bundle of nerves, the place she herself had been too shy to touch.

She resisted the urge to gasp, completely unable to take her eyes off of him, off of what he was doing to her.

"Mmm..." she heard him murmur, and the sound thrilled her beyond anything she could ever imagine.

His tongue was teasing her, playing with her, taunting her. Without even realizing it, she lowered her hand and gripped a handful of his hair, offering herself up to him, yearning for more.

He took her most sensitive flesh into his mouth, and pleasure unfurled from deep inside of her, blossoming outward, spreading through every part of her being. She felt her entire body tremble as his lips worked together with his tongue, flicking over her in steady pulses, only to spread her wet folds, allowing his tongue to sink into her.

"Oh…" she moaned loudly, biting her lip. She didn't know how much more of this she could take before coming undone right there, with her thigh resting on top of him and with a fistful of his locks between her fingers.

Then something happened. It felt as if every single nerve inside of her clenched, only to explode in a molten rush of heat and pleasure. He tenderly sucked her swollen pearl into his mouth, taking into himself her every tremor, her every beat.

When he pulled away, she was still shivering slightly. He looked at her with a sense of pure, unadulterated pleasure, and she imagined she looked the same. He got up without taking his eyes off of her. His fingers brushed against the wetness on his lips, then he leaned in and kissed her, allowing her to taste herself.

Skin to skin, breath to breath, she thought to herself with a smile.

He smiled back. She thought he might speak, say something half-clever or self-protective. But he didn't. Instead, he only bid her good night, then disappeared behind the doors that she thought were there to separate them, but now, she knew better.

For a door that was meant to separate could always become a door that united…

***

The morning light was unusually unkind. It was not harsh exactly, but simply revealing in a manner that was determined to expose every emotion Catharine had carefully kept sealed.

She decided to keep her eyes low. Her fingers rested lightly on her teacup, movements precise, composed. She said nothing as Isadora spoke of nothing in particular: the weather, the state of the rose garden, a new French bonnet she'd seen in a magazine. Catharine nodded at all the right moments, offering polite commentary when required.

And yet she felt *bare.*

Last night lived beneath her skin like a fever. The heat of his lips still ghosted between her thighs. She had slept eventually, but not deeply. She'd risen before dawn, slipped back into her room without anyone seeing, and sat for nearly an hour at her dressing table, trying to reassemble the mask she wore so well.

And now here she was, sipping tea and pretending she hadn't come undone in his arms. She felt his glance even before she saw it.

Alaric sat at the head of the table with a newspaper unfolded in one hand, the other cradling a coffee cup he hadn't touched in several minutes. He didn't stare, but he also didn't *not* look. There was a sharpness to his gaze that felt subtle and unmistakable. It grazed her like a fingertip across bare skin. It took all of her conscious effort not to look in his direction.

Isadora set down her fork with a faint clink and tilted her head. "You look tired, Catharine," she said, too lightly. "There's a dullness about your eyes. I hope you aren't falling ill."

Catharine's spine stiffened. She raised her cup again, hiding behind the rim. "It was only a poor night's sleep."

"Restlessness," Alaric murmured without looking up. "It'll do that to a person. Especially when it strikes late."

Catharine nearly choked on her tea. She covered it with a gentle cough, then set the cup down with exquisite care.

"Must be the change in weather," she said coolly, though her ears burned.

Across the table, Isadora's brows lifted in curiosity. "Mm," she said, drawing out the sound. "Strange. I slept wonderfully."

"Well, evidently not everyone was so fortunate, Izza," Alaric replied, turning a page in his paper.

His voice was smooth as ever, but Catharine could feel that undercurrent of mischief, that simmering satisfaction he barely tried to hide. And beneath it… warmth? The quiet kind. It was not teasing to mock her, but to see if she'd meet his glance and respond in kind. She couldn't, not with Isadora sitting there like a cat with a bowl of cream.

"Well," Isadora said breezily, dabbing her mouth with her napkin, "perhaps you should take a tonic. Or a walk. Fresh air does wonders for the nerves."

Catharine took a long breath. "My nerves are perfectly intact."

Isadora's eyes sparkled. "Oh, I don't doubt it. But still… you never know what lingers after a restless night. And I know just what you need: a trip to town."

Catharine arched a brow. "For what purpose?"

"For my reputation," Isadora said playfully. "And yours, by association. I need a dress."

"Don't you have enough dresses?" Alaric interfered.

Isadora pouted. "I have statements in fabric. What I need is a weapon."

Alaric almost chuckled. Catharine could see the almost invisible tug of his lips, but he managed to remain calm and composed, as always. And that was that. Less than an hour later, she and Isadora were inside Madame Lenoir's townhouse-turned-dressmaker's atelier, which was a refined little shop of quiet luxury and sharp-nosed apprentices. The air smelled of pressed muslin and violet powder. Bolts of silk spilled over chaise longues in shades of oyster, midnight, and pale amethyst. A tray of lace samples glinted in the filtered morning sun, delicate as frost.

Isadora moved through the room like a general securing a battalion to win not only the battle but the entire war. Catharine followed more slowly, letting her fingers skim the edge of a bolt of dove-grey satin. Her thoughts wandered to last night, despite herself. She couldn't stop thinking about the feel of Alaric's lips on her skin and the warmth that had not left her since.

"I like this one for you," Isadora said suddenly, lifting a length of deep forest green and pressing it against Catharine's shoulder. "It makes your eyes look like you see *everything*, even when you pretend not to."

Catharine tilted her head with amusement on her lips. "You're determined to make me memorable?"

"Memorable is good," Isadora agreed. "Untouchable is better."

Before Catharine could ask what she meant, a smooth, slightly too amused voice drifted towards them.

"Ah, the lovely Lady Vale," a man drawled. "One married into the family, the other one born into it."

"Lord Blackmoor," Isadora greeted him, but the politeness in her voice was demanded, not given freely. Catharine merely bowed her head in greeting silently. She had been introduced to the man once, briefly, and that was enough to know that she did not like him one whit.

He stood just inside the doorway with his gloved hands folded behind his back. His smile was all surface. It was mocking without edge, charm without sincerity. His eyes flicked from Catharine to the fabric, then back to her face.

"Shopping for the occasion?" he asked, his lips curving like a fox's. "I do admire your efficiency. You haven't been married a whole month, and you are already very… ambitious."

Catharine went still. The remark wasn't overtly cruel. However, it landed with quiet, poisonous precision, like all veiled insults did.

Isadora, on the other hand, wasn't still. She stepped forward, slightly between Catharine and Lord Blackmoor, like a shield.

"May I remind you that you are speaking to the Marchioness of Ravensedge, which makes her ten ranks above the petty provocations of lesser men."

Lord Blackmoor blinked, not expecting such defence, but Isadora wasn't finished. "As for ambition, it is highly advisable for some lords to mind their throats more than their tongues. Reputations can be stitched together. Necks, however, are less forgiving."

No one moved for what seemed to be an entire eternity. Then Lord Blackmoor offered a shallow bow, not quite mocking but far from a respectful greeting of two ladies.

"Always a pleasure, ladies." Upon those words, he turned, his amusement trailing behind him even more than his cheap cologne.

Catharine stared at the bolt of green silk in her hands, her grip just a shade too tight. She turned to Isadora with a smile. "That was… something. Thank you."

Isadora grinned. "Don't thank me. The man is a nuisance." She took the bolt of green silk from Catharine's hand and put it away. "We need something... worth stabbing a man over."

This time, Catharine couldn't resist chuckling. But still, even through the laughs, a sense of dread remained.

Chapter Fourteen

The drawing room had never looked more polished. Vases were overflowing with fresh hothouse blooms, and the porcelain was gleaming like bone in the afternoon light. Tea had been served precisely at four, the silver pot catching the firelight in soft flashes as the footman poured. Everything in the household, from the plump cushions to the fire's height, had been adjusted in anticipation.

The Duke and Duchess of Kingswell had arrived.

Catharine sat poised beside her sister Eliza on the settee, as a plate of untouched seed cake balanced delicately in her lap. Across from them, Rhys Ashbourne, her brother-in-law and the formidable duke himself, spoke in his usual clipped tones, which were measured but never indifferent.

"I understand your steward managed to reverse the grain tariffs in Devonshire," Alaric said with one arm draped across the back of his chair. His tone was neutral, but there was a glint of something wry behind it. "A rare miracle."

Rhys gave the ghost of a smile. "No miracle, just endurance... and a little blackmail."

Eliza gave a soft gasp, which was feigned but elegant. "Rhys."

He didn't look at her. "You married *me*, darling, not a curate."

Catharine glanced from her sister to the duke and back again with a slight tug at her mouth betraying her amusement. Eliza always did have a talent for softening the sharpest of edges, even her husband's.

Alaric leaned forward slightly to pour another cup of tea. His movements were smooth and unhurried, although he did not look in Catharine's direction even once. "I imagine endurance is what it takes to keep a seat these days. Especially with the Committee pressing every landowner with two coins and a conscience."

Rhys took the tea with a nod. "And your seat, Ravensedge?" he asked lightly. "How long do they expect you to remain silent before they decide you're tame?"

Catharine's fingers tightened on her teacup. But Alaric didn't blink.

"I've never pretended to be tame," he said. "But I know when to wait."

Rhys studied him for a long moment, then gave a single, deliberate nod. "Good."

There was a pause. Then Eliza, in her usual gentle tyranny, turned to Catharine and broke the silence. "You've grown thin."

Catharine arched a brow. "That's what you open with after a year apart?"

"I'm your sister. If I can't insult you, who can?"

"I was under the impression it was half of London."

Eliza smiled as the two sisters huddled together with the men, turning to their own topics.

"You've done well here," Eliza commented. "The staff likes you."

"They're paid to," Catharine reminded her.

Her comment made her sister chuckle. "That never made them like *me*."

Catharine couldn't help but join in. Seeing her sister again made her feel slightly more at ease, though she couldn't help but feel overlooked by her own husband. By the time the supper was served in the smaller dining room, the soft elegance of the afternoon had started to fray at the edges. Not visibly, of course, but something had shifted.

The candles burned steadily, the roast was perfectly done, the wine flowed. And yet every time Catharine reached for her glass, she could feel it: the strange, brittle silence between herself and her husband. She had to admit that he hadn't looked at her properly… not since *that* night.

She tried telling herself that it was nothing, that men like him were always more comfortable in action than aftermath. But even when she allowed for that, it didn't explain the careful distance in his voice, the way he listened to Eliza's light conversation without offering more than a few clipped replies. And when his gaze did cross hers, it was brief, almost like a mistake. The space between them at the table had never felt wider.

"Do you mean to ride out tomorrow, my lord?" Rhys asked casually, breaking the quiet.

"I do," Alaric said, with his eyes still on his plate. "There's been some flooding in the western fields."

Catharine sipped her wine. "You could have someone else do it. Why would a marquess be trudging through mud to impress tenants?"

"Better mud than drawing rooms," he murmured, not looking at her.

The words weren't sharp, but they brushed against her, enough to leave a mark.

Eliza glanced between them, her brows lifting in that subtle, maddening way of hers. "The two of you truly are well-suited. You bicker with such grace."

Catharine smiled a flash of teeth. "We don't bicker. That would require him to speak to me."

A silence followed, more telling than any outburst.

Rhys cleared his throat. "And how fares the east orchard? I'd heard rumours of blight last year."

Alaric answered smoothly, with statistics and facts, not once looking her way. The air grew tight in Catharine's lungs.

Why won't you look at me?

She'd kissed him back. She'd said yes. And still it felt like she'd done something wrong, like he regretted it. Or worse, like she'd made herself too vulnerable, and he now pitied her for it. She could not bear that.

When the footman offered more wine, she declined with a nod too sharp to be polite.

"Catharine," Eliza said with feigned innocence, "you haven't said a word about your birthday."

Catharine blinked. "That's because there's nothing to say."

"You always hated the attention," Eliza mused. "But now that you're married, surely you'll let yourself be celebrated at least *once*."

Catharine cut a glance at Alaric. He didn't react. He didn't so much as shift in his chair.

"No, I don't need anything like that," she said, hoping for a change of topic.

Her fingers clenched in her lap beneath the table. Because the truth was... the silence hurt. And it hurt more than she'd expected, more than she would ever admit.

If he had regretted touching her, he might have at least had the decency to say so. But then again, she knew he was a man who had learned to endure pain in silence, just as she had.

And perhaps neither of them quite knew how to speak when it wasn't out of strategy or necessity...

**

The men had retreated to the library, leaving leather and the scent of brandy trailing behind them. Their voices, now low and muffled, hummed faintly through the walls.

Catharine remained behind in the drawing room, her fingers worrying the edge of her napkin as the fire crackled softly. Eliza sat beside her on the chaise with her posture relaxed, but her eyes far too knowing.

"What was all that about, Catharine?" Eliza asked gently. "It looked like the storm before a worse storm."

"Oh, Eliza." Catharine inhaled deeply. "It's... everything."

She glanced towards the door, then away. The candlelight played against the fine china on the sideboard, glinting over the crystal decanter left untouched. It did nothing to distract her.

"Eliza..." She felt hesitant talking about this, but this was her sister, her confidant. "Something happened between Alaric and me."

Eliza blinked. "Happened as in...?"

"Well—" Catherina blushed, not really certain how to go about explaining this. "You know... what happens between a husband and a wife..."

"You mean, he has made love to you?" Eliza asked without any pardon.

"Oh, no, no, not *that*." Catharine was hasty to dissuade her sister. "He has just... you know..." She paused, pointing down between her legs.

"Ooh, *that!*" Eliza chuckled. "And did you like it?"

"Yes, I... I did." Catharine nodded, feeling confused and embarrassed but willing to understand what she had done wrong.

"When was that?"

"The night before you arrived."

"Did it happen more than once?"

"No," Catharine confessed, biting her lip nervously. "And that's just it... Nothing else has happened since then. There was no word about it, no acknowledgement beyond civility."

Eliza hummed, the sound almost amused. "Well. That does explain the strange mood at supper. And the way you kept stabbing the potatoes."

Catharine groaned and dropped her face into her hands. "God, was it *that* obvious?"

"Only to me. Rhys thinks everyone is tense by nature."

There was a pause.

"I thought," Catharine said slowly, "that it might... mean something. I was hoping that he'd say something. Or at least *look* at me. But it's as if he regrets it, or as if I made some mistake."

Eliza's face softened. "You didn't."

"No, I let myself want something," she admitted. "*That's* the mistake."

Eliza reached for her hand, ungloved and warm. "Or maybe it's just *new*. For both of you. He doesn't strike me as a man who knows what to do with feelings that don't fit inside a command."

Catharine gave a dry laugh. "Neither do I."

Eliza studied her for a long moment. "Then don't expect too much, too soon. Some men need time to understand their own minds. Others need a little... direction."

Catharine looked at her. "You mean I should chase him?"

"Good Lord, no." Eliza smiled, then leaned in with a conspirator's gleam in her eye. "Make *him* chase *you*—if that is what you want, of course."

Catharine arched a brow. "And how, precisely, do I do that without looking absurd?"

"Start by being the woman he watched all through supper," Eliza said simply. "Be sharp, elusive, and most importantly, unbothered."

"But I was none of those things. I was brittle and sarcastic."

"And he noticed," Eliza replied. "Trust me. You've already lit the match. Now stop staring at the fire and walk away. Let *him* follow."

Could she? Could she play indifference when every fiber of her wanted answers, closeness, something to anchor her in this new uncertainty? She wasn't certain.

However, she wasn't allowed to linger in that uncertainty for too long because the men returned.

"Did you miss us so terribly you had to come back and interrupt us?" Eliza teased her husband.

"Yes." Rhys nodded, amused but without a smile. "That is *exactly* what happened." He was still standing up when he continued. "It has gotten pretty late, my dear. I think we should let our hosts rest, lest we take advantage of their good will."

The ladies stood up at his words, and several minutes later, Catharine and her sister were standing by the front hall, watching from a polite distance as the two men exchanged their final words.

"Your tenant charters are tight," Rhys was saying in a steady and professional tone of voice. "You'll want to loosen those margins before they resent you for doing too much too fast."

Alaric nodded once. "I appreciate the advice. And the candour."

Rhys adjusted his gloves. "I judge men by their mind, not by the papers sold in coffeehouses."

Alaric's mouth tugged into something faint. It was not a smile, but close. "Then I expect we'll get on."

Eliza, already cloaked and radiant even by candlelight, turned to Catharine and gave her hand a squeeze. "I'll write."

Their embrace was long and tender. A touch of perfume, a whisper of hair against her cheek, and then the doors opened, allowing the night air to rush in, after which their carriage rattled into the darkness.

The hall fell into a hush, and the footmen dispersed. Catharine turned around only to see Alaric standing several paces away. They were alone, and still, he said nothing.

She met his gaze. Or at least, she tried to, but his eyes did not settle on hers. Instead, they slid past.

"I'll be out early," he said at last. "The west fields need surveying."

"Of course," she replied, voice level. "Your tenants deserve attention."

He paused then, just long enough for her hope to catch before letting it fall again.

"Good night, Lady Ravensedge."

He bowed his head slightly and left her standing there. The house felt cold now. Or perhaps it was just her, feeling the return of that familiar hollowness beneath the ribs, the one she thought she'd started to outgrow.

She climbed the staircase slowly, with her chin held high, just as she had after every other disappointment in her life. And yet... this one hurt differently because it hadn't been the failure she feared.

It was hope.

Chapter Fifteen

Alaric was used to being looked at.

War had made him visible. Scandal had made him notorious. But this evening, there was a different quality to the stares that surrounded him at the ballroom of Lord and Lady Kensington. People smiled too widely, stood too tall, and whispered just a little too loudly behind painted fans. Theirs was a curiosity dressed up as civility, suspicion softened by feigned admiration, for they weren't just watching him. No. They were watching them both.

He offered his arm to Catharine as they entered, and she took it without hesitation, her fingers light against the sleeve of his coat. Her posture was impeccable, and there was the barest of smiles playing on her lips like a secret she had no intention of sharing.

For a moment, even he forgot to breathe.

Her gown was not the sort of thing she had worn before. They were not the soft, elegant shades Catharine usually chose for herself. This was a bold and deliberate statement in the form of a deep garnet silk that clung to her waist and flared like flame at her skirts, offset by dark embroidery that traced the bodice like ivy.

It was not a dress for blending in. It was a declaration, and it fit her like a challenge fit a sword.

They moved together through the entryway as the sea of murmurs parted before them. He caught Isadora's eye across the room, and he saw the faintest curl of satisfaction at the corner of her mouth as she raised her glass in a wordless toast. She obviously approved of what Catharine was doing.

As for himself... he said nothing, but something in his chest tightened seeing her so desirable. It had been maddeningly difficult keeping his distance from her for the very simple reason that he couldn't act with composure in her presence. She had an effect on him the likes of which he could never have dreamed of. Hearing her call out his name five nights ago had been a siren's call that he shouldn't have answered. Now he had heard her song, and like Odysseus, he had to keep himself tied to the mast so that he wouldn't rush into her arms and lose his head.

He'd expected her to keep to the shadows tonight. He had expected her to be reserved, distant, to be the version of herself she showed when she felt cornered. Instead, she stood at his side not as an ornament but as an equal, and therefore something far more dangerous: a woman who had nothing left to lose.

He leaned in just enough to be heard over the swell of strings. "I was under the impression that I married a woman fond of restraint."

Her eyes didn't leave the room. "Restraint is for dull evenings and men who do not speak when speaking is necessary."

Just as he was about to retort something, the host and the hostess approached them, offering appropriate pleasantries in the form of a greeting.

"Ah, Lord and Lady Ravensedge, what a pleasure." Lord Kensington took the lead.

"It is a magical ball." Catharine smiled with a curtsey. "Your decorations are absolutely magnificent."

"Oh, you are such a sweetheart for saying so," Lady Kensington chirped cheerfully, in a voice like taffeta.

After a few more exchanged words, the hosts continued into the throng of polite predators and powdered charm. Alaric tried not to look around, not to notice a countess whispering behind a fan, a viscount bowing too low, someone from the House of Lords staring as if trying to spot the monster behind the man.

Let them look, he thought to himself. *Let them whisper.*

That was when Eliza appeared at Catharine's side like a breeze slipping through an open window.

"Forgive me," she said, her smile almost too innocent to trust. "But I'm stealing your wife. There's a duchess desperate to meet her. Something about scandal, beauty, and a taste for rebellion."

Catharine arched a brow but allowed herself to be led away, glancing back just once, in one last flicker of acknowledgment that might have meant *wait for me*—or might have also meant *watch me.*

Alaric did both.

Catharine moved through the room like she belonged to it, like she'd been born not just to survive in society but to bend it subtly to her will. Grace and calculation walked beside her in every step. She knew how to incline her head just enough to suggest intimacy, how to let her smile hover before releasing it in full. It wasn't flirtation. No. He had seen women yield flirtation, but never with such skill. This was something else. This was pure power.

He stood near the tall windows, watching her. He was also watching the way laughter bubbled from her lips at something the Marchioness of Harbury said. He noticed the flick of her fingers as she gestured with a glass in hand. He gritted his teeth when three different men circled just a bit too near, hovering like moths who hadn't yet realised the flame would kill them.

He couldn't deny it, especially not to himself, that she was radiant. And *his*. But she didn't look like *his*, not with that garnet silk like poured wine across her skin, not with that laugh that wasn't for him, not with her hand lightly touching Eliza's arm or her words sparking delight in a circle of women who had once whispered about her behind their gloves.

Tonight, he'd expected her to retreat in public and allow him to lead. Instead, she had risen, and the entire ballroom noticed it, especially the men. He saw it in the way they glanced at her, then glanced again... longer this time. He saw it in the smug curve of another man's smile as he bowed, in the way one lord leaned in a little too close for comfort during conversation.

Alaric's jaw clenched. His hand curled loosely at his side.

He didn't belong in this world any longer. He never had, not really. And now he watched her move through that same world as if it had never tried to chew her up and spit her out. She didn't need protection. She didn't need his name. And yet she had it. He himself had *her,* but... for how long? With her being so alive that every man in the room seemed ready to offer the admiration he himself kept locked behind silence and restraint, he couldn't know anything.

He'd touched her once. He had kissed her like a drowning man. And since then, he'd punished them both for it.

He didn't realise he'd gone still until Gainsworth appeared at his shoulder, all teeth and amusement.

"Well, well," his friend drawled, swirling his drink. "It seems your wife's glacier has thawed."

"It would seem so," Alaric murmured reluctantly, not taking his eyes from Catharine.

That damned Lord Huntley keeps standing too close to her, he couldn't stop thinking.

"Your wife is truly radiant tonight," Dorian continued. "Positively bewitching. Only... third glass of champagne, voice as bright as any debutante, and with a crowd of men hanging on her every word. She is not quite the woman who glared daggers at your wedding."

Alaric didn't answer. He was too focused on what was happening across the ballroom. Catharine stood like firelight in a storm. She was laughing, with that garnet dress scandalously perfect against her skin. Her hand touched someone's arm too lightly to be innocent, and the men around her were practically buzzing with hunger disguised as charm. One of them said something that made her laugh, and her head tilted just enough to bare the line of her neck.

Something in Alaric snapped. He was moving before he had time to think better of it. Champagne sloshed in glasses as he cut across the floor, no longer caring for pretence. Her laugh reached him just as he arrived, bright and a little too loose.

"Catharine," he said firmly, taking her elbow with the tips of his fingers.

She turned, her cheeks flushed from wine and attention.

"Oh, Alaric." Her smile didn't falter, but he saw the flicker of wariness behind it. "I was just—"

He didn't let her finish. "We need a word."

She blinked. "Can it not wait?"

"No."

Without waiting for another question, he guided her through the nearby crowd towards the door, then down a short corridor lit only by sconces and the hush of muffled strings. He proceeded to open the door to a drawing room and stepped aside to let her enter. The moment the door shut, she turned on him.

"You made a scene."

"*You* made a *spectacle.*"

Her eyes narrowed. "I was speaking and laughing. Or have you forgotten what it felt like to enjoy yourself?"

"You are drunk," he snapped. "And surrounded by men who couldn't decide whether to flirt or devour you."

"I'm not yours to manage."

"You're my wife."

"Convenient of you to remember now," she bit back. "You certainly haven't acted like it."

His breath caught. That comment landed.

"Why now, Alaric?" she pressed. "Because I danced with someone else? Because I laughed too long at a joke you didn't hear? Or is it because I was finally more than a strategic accessory at your side?"

He watched the heave of her full chest, the colour in her cheeks, and finally, the hurt in her eyes that she tried to pass off as rage.

"You were..." He swallowed. "You were undone."

"And what of it?" she demanded. "Do you only want me as long as I'm perfectly composed and quiet? Is that what makes me safe to want?"

"I didn't say that."

"You didn't have to," she said coldly. "You haven't looked at me since that night. At least, not in the way that matters. You kissed me like I was the only thing holding you together, and then vanished into silence. So tell me, Lord Ravensedge. Do *you* care what *they* see?"

The question hung in the air. He stepped closer, not touching her... yet.

"I care what they see," he said angrily. "Because I know what they *want*."

"And you think I'll let them have it?" she said, incredulous. "That I want their eyes?" She shook her head in more disbelief. "I don't want to be looked at, Alaric. I want to be *seen*."

Her voice was tight with emotion and pride, defence sharpened by old wounds. Only he could barely hear her words anymore. How could he, when she was standing so close, when the blood was pounding in his ears?

He didn't think. He *lunged*.

One hand gripped her waist, the other tangled in her hair, and his mouth crushed down on hers with the force of every word he hadn't said. She gasped, half in shock, half in protest, but it died on his lips. Her hands braced against his chest, uncertain at first, and then they clutched his coat... fiercely. He kissed her like he was still angry, like the only way to win the argument was to unmake it entirely.

Her back hit the wall with a soft thud, and she moaned into the kiss. It was just one moan, muffled and unguarded, and it shattered something in him. Her fingers curled into his shoulders. Her body arched, desperate and furious and utterly alive beneath his touch.

He pulled back barely an inch, breathing harshly, with his forehead resting against hers.

"Is that what you want?" he asked roughly. "A husband who sees you only when he's furious?"

She looked back at him, her eyes burning. "I want a husband who doesn't run the moment he feels something real."

He didn't answer. He kissed her again instead. And this time, she kissed him back like she meant to punish him for making her feel so much, like she meant to burn him alive.

His fingers swept over her as if she were something precious, something he never wished to let go of. His hand gripped her breast through the corset, pulling the material down as far as it would go. A peach-coloured nipple slipped out of the forbidden fabric of the gown, and he couldn't resist trailing an invisible path of kisses down her collarbone to the exposed soft flesh of her breast.

"Oh..." she moaned loudly again, biting her lower lip. She gasped when he took her nipple into his mouth, tugging at it gently.

He used the heat of his mouth, the wetness of his tongue, wanting to chase away all the fears she had that he didn't want her again and again. He wanted to make her feel beautiful, desired, to cover her body in an explosion of all the senses.

He wanted to taste her again, to lift the hem of her devilish gown that had started all of this and bring her to pleasure just like the previous time, but he knew they were risking a lot. Still, he couldn't stop. His hands kept gripping her tighter and tighter with his lips locked onto her fragrant skin. Her scent kept teasing him as his tongue circled the puckered bud of her nipple.

Everything about her was sheer perfection. His lips found hers once more, delving into her mouth, his fingers playing with her nipple, tormenting her into a frenzy. His own manhood roared from the constraint of his trousers. There was nothing he wanted more than to claim her right here, right now, to feel the cataclysmic warmth of her most sensual place.

But then he felt her push him away. It wasn't hard, but enough to break the kiss and make him stumble half a step back.

She stood in front of him with her lips red and swollen, her chest rising and falling beneath the curve of her gown, and her hair slightly undone from where his hands had been. Her wild, dark eyes locked onto his, and something in them made his mouth go dry.

She looked like no lady he had ever known. She looked like something half-feral, a wood nymph dressed in silk and fire, trembling not from fear but from restraint.

A dozen things came to his lips: apologies, explanations, something, *anything* to make sense of what had just happened. But he couldn't form the words. He was still caught in her gaze, dizzy with the taste of her, the echo of her voice when she'd said: *I want a husband who doesn't run.*

Catharine said nothing. She pulled up her gown, then simply turned and gracefully walked out the door, leaving only the ghost of her perfume in the air behind her.

He didn't follow because he wasn't certain if following her meant ruin or salvation.

Chapter Sixteen

The moment the door shut behind her, Catharine barely had time to collect breath or thought.

"There you are."

Isadora's voice cut through the corridor like a blade dressed in lace. Before Catharine could utter a word, a gloved hand closed firmly around her wrist.

"I—Isadora—"

"Not here."

Isadora tugged her briskly through a side hallway and into a small powder room tucked discreetly near the card salon. The scent of rosewater and starch clung to the air, and the delicate murmur of society dulled behind the door as it clicked shut, providing at least a semblance of safety from prying eyes.

Isadora exhaled loudly. Then she folded her arms across her bodice as her eyes took in every dishevelled detail about Catharine's appearance: the loosened chignon, the shifted neckline of her gown, the slight flush on her cheeks that rouge couldn't have created on its own, and the unmistakable bloom of her lips.

Isadora's brow arched. "Well?" Her voice was too even and all too knowing.

"It's... not what you think," Catharine managed to muster, making her way for the looking glass at once. Her fingers rushed to tame her hair and to pull the neckline back into its proper place.

"Oh?" Isadora leaned back against the wall, looking utterly unconvinced. "Because what I *think* is that my cousin just cornered his wife in a private room, and you've only just escaped with your corset still half-laced."

"I'm perfectly laced," Catharine muttered, refusing to meet her eyes.

"Not in spirit, darling."

Catharine turned sharply. "It was nothing."

Isadora tilted her head. "Nothing doesn't leave your lips looking like that or your voice sounding like someone just kissed the breath out of you."

Catharine swallowed heavily. It provided a moment for her thoughts.

"I'm fine," she said tightly, tugging a pin back into place with more force than necessary.

Isadora stepped closer, her irreverent grin softening into something quieter. "You know, I've seen scandal. Heaven knows I've even *been* scandal on a few occasions. But you"— she gestured gently towards her—"you don't seem to me the sort of person who does anything without intention, which tells me whatever just happened… matters."

Catharine hesitated. She stared at her reflection, at the woman in the mirror who looked not like a wife or a lady of rank but someone just a shade undone, someone who had kissed her husband as if it meant something and then fled as if it couldn't.

"*He* kissed *me*," she said finally, as if that changed anything.

Isadora's eyes gleamed with amusement. "Is that so?"

"It wasn't supposed to happen."

"But it did, and you're glowing like a stained-glass window about to crack."

Catharine turned away from the mirror and sat on the small bench beside it, fingers clenching the fabric of her skirt. "He said nothing after. Just let me go. And I... left."

"You didn't slap him, so it couldn't have been terrible," Isadora offered lightly.

Catharine's eyes flicked up. "No."

"Besides," Isadora chirped, "he is your husband. He does have a right to kiss you if he wants to, you know."

"What if I don't want to?" Catharine pouted.

"Well, don't you?" Isadora asked playfully, although the answer was clear as daylight.

Catharine stood, composed once more but still burning beneath the skin.

"Help me fix this," she murmured.

"Your hair, or your heart?" Isadora teased, reaching for a comb.

Catharine gave a tight smile. "One at a time."

Isadora worked swiftly. Her fingers moved through Catharine's loosened chignon, tucking strands with the efficiency of someone used to mending appearances before questions could form. She reached for a comb, then a ribbon from her own reticule. It was navy blue, understated, the kind of elegance that deflected scrutiny.

Catharine sat stiffly on the velvet-cushioned bench, trying to ignore the throb in her lips and the fast rhythm in her chest. Her bodice had been straightened, her hair retamed, and her gloves rebuttoned. But it still felt like something in her had come undone and remained that way.

Isadora's voice cut gently into the quiet. "Hold still."

"I *am* holding still."

"You're vibrating like a tuning fork."

"I'm fine."

"Liar."

Catharine gave a half-laugh, half-sigh. "You're enjoying this far too much, admit it."

"Of course I am," Isadora chuckled. "It's not every day I get to rescue a marchioness from the ruins of her own dignity."

Catharine arched a brow. "And do you consider this a rescue?"

"No," Isadora said, reaching for a pin. "This is reconstruction."

She worked a final twist into Catharine's hair, then stepped back and surveyed her handiwork with a nod of approval.

"There. Proper and lovely. Only the keenest observer would guess you were just ravished against a drawing room wall."

"I was not—"

"Oh, please. The back of your gown says otherwise." Isadora gave a wink and handed her a mirror.

Catharine peered at her reflection. She looked strangely composed again, but her eyes betrayed her. They glinted with something she hadn't seen there in years. It was heat, maybe, or hunger. Or perhaps something far more dangerous.

Isadora opened the door slightly, peeking into the corridor. "All clear. No gossiping dowagers or meddling aunts in sight."

Catharine stood and smoothed her skirts, slipping the mask of cool composure over her features once more.

"Back to battle, then," she said.

"Back to the ballroom," Isadora corrected, linking their arms. "Battle comes later."

When they returned to the ballroom, everything glittered exactly as before. The chandeliers were dripping with light, the music was lilting through murmurs and laughter, a thousand lives were spinning in satin and scandal. But for Catharine, the room felt irrevocably changed, and all because *he* was watching.

Alaric was standing near the tall windows at the far end of the room, half in shadow, his posture deceptively still. His dark coat cut a clean, severe line through the golden haze of candlelight. He was speaking to someone, but his attention wasn't there. It was on *her*. And when their eyes met, something in her stomach dropped.

At his side stood Lord Dorian Gainsworth, unmistakable in his tailored indifference, sipping something golden from a slim crystal flute. The two men were as opposite as sin and silence: Dorian all flashing grin and commentary, Alaric unreadable as stone. Isadora, of course, led them directly towards the pair. Catharine had just enough time to brace herself before they arrived.

"Gentlemen," Isadora commented lightly, giving Lord Gainsworth a mockingly shallow curtsey. "I trust the ballroom remained intact in our absence."

Gainsworth turned with a lazy smile. "Lady Isadora. I was beginning to worry the chandeliers had swallowed you whole."

"I do like to keep you guessing," she said, too sweetly. "It's good for your constitution."

Gainsworth chuckled. "Ah, so this is a concern. How flattering. I thought it was merely your disdain dressed up in ribbon."

Isadora leaned forward, her eyes sparkling at him. "I find that if I tie up my disdain well enough, men like you mistake it for attention."

Lord Gainsworth's grin widened. "Touché."

The tension between them shimmered. It was stuck somewhere between half flirtation and half fencing match. Catharine glanced briefly between them, surprised by the electricity sparking so openly. She didn't think Isadora was someone easily caught off guard in any conversation... but Lord Gainsworth had a way of baiting people just enough to pull them in.

Alaric, on his part, had said little. However, the sharp line of his jaw and the silence that pressed tight between his shoulders spoke louder than any words ever could. The mood had shifted. One moment, they stood amid music and mirrors, the glittering pulse of society in full swing. The next, his voice cut through it like a blade.

"We're leaving."

There was no raised tone, no visible temper. It was a simple, calm command that he expected to be heard and obeyed.

Catharine blinked. "Now?"

He didn't answer, only offered his arm. Across the ballroom, heads turned, making conversations falter and fans still in mid-motion. Some smiled behind gloved hands, while others whispered. A few, bolder still, looked between them with open curiosity, eager to carve a new rumour from the air left behind.

But Alaric didn't glance at a single one. Neither did she.

Catharine placed her hand on his arm, composed and cool. She behaved as if she didn't still taste his kiss, as if her gown wasn't slightly creased from where his hands had clutched her only an hour before, as if her heart hadn't begun beating entirely too fast the moment he entered the room and never quite slowed. That was how they walked through the parting crowd in silence.

The carriage waited at the bottom of the stairs, sleek and black. Its lanterns glowed soft amber in the night. A footman opened the door. Alaric helped her in without a word. Inside, the silence pressed in again like quicksand, threatening to swallow them alive.

He sat across from her. She could feel his stare, even when she didn't meet it. The crush of her skirts between them seemed suddenly intimate. Her hands were folded tightly in her lap, but her pulse betrayed her.

Outside the windows, London slipped past. The gas lamps were glowing, and the night was chilly and dusted with the silvery light of the moon. But inside the carriage, everything burned.

Chapter Seventeen

She was untouched by it all, untouched by *him.*

He couldn't understand it. She behaved as if hours ago, he hadn't pressed her against the wall and kissed her until she shook, as if none of it mattered. That quiet, deliberate composure needled him.

Alaric's jaw flexed as he studied her from beneath lowered lids. Every inch of her had returned to its pristine order: not a strand of hair out of place, not a ribbon crooked, not a single emotion permitted to linger on her carefully arranged face.

Except he knew better. He'd felt the way she trembled when he touched her. He'd also heard the way she said his name. And still, she sat there like marble: cool, polished, and unbreakable.

He looked away, a low breath escaping him. This was becoming untenable. The boundaries they'd set, those same boundaries which were once silent, mutual, and necessary, were already bending. Another night like this, another kiss like that, and they'd snap completely. And what would be left? Nothing safe. Nothing clean. Nothing he could control.

Real emotions had no place in a marriage born of necessity. He had married Catharine to repair what remained of his reputation, to give her protection, name, and the illusion of stability. That was all. That was their ironclad agreement.

And yet... That kiss had undone something in both of them. Now, in the soft dark of the carriage, he could feel the remnants of it curling in the air between them like smoke from a dying flame.

They had barely crossed the threshold of Ravensedge Hall before he spoke. "This cannot happen again."

His voice was not angry or cruel, just precise and cold with the edge of steel held too long in the fire. Catharine paused at the foot of the grand staircase, her hand still resting lightly on the banister. She turned to face him as the soft lamplight brushed across the sharp angle of her porcelain cheekbone.

"Oh?" she said. Her tone was maddeningly light.

He stared at her. "It was reckless."

Catharine blinked slowly, as if struggling to recall what precisely he was referring to. "You'll have to be more specific, my lord. Recklessness is so common in our household these days."

Alaric's jaw clenched. She knew *exactly* what he meant. And she was doing it on purpose, acting as though nothing had passed between them in that quiet chamber, as if there had been no kiss, no heat, no wild, furious entanglement of hands and mouths and breathless need. Now it seemed that all that existed was this maddening poise.

Her composure stung more than any slap could have, much more than the worst insult whispered at any gentlemen's club.

"I'm being serious, Catharine."

"I can tell." She offered a faint, unbothered smile. "It's very impressive."

He took a step closer, slow and deliberate, as if trying to read what lay behind that impenetrable mask of hers. "That wasn't part of our arrangement."

"I wasn't aware we had anything quite so formal." Her gaze lifted to his. "But don't worry. I assure you that I have no intention of becoming sentimental."

His breath caught in his throat. It was the tone that she used. It was the same tone she knew she had been using to keep the world at bay, just like he had. But hearing it from her, now directed at *him,* dug under his skin like shards of broken glass.

Even through this, she still looked calm, as though he hadn't come undone in the taste of her mouth and her skin.

He stepped back. She inclined her head slightly, a gesture so effortlessly cool he wanted to shake her just to prove she did feel something. But instead, she gave a quiet, practiced curtsey.

"Good night, my lord."

Then she turned and ascended the stairs, graceful as ever, without a single backward glance. She escaped, just like sleep had escaped him that night.

Alaric lay on his back in the dim hush of his bedchamber, the fire long reduced to embers, and the candle burned low on the desk across the room. Yet no amount of darkness dulled the clarity of the memory that haunted him.

Her mouth on his jaw... the sound of her breath catching when he touched her face... the feel of her fingers twisting in his coat as if she'd finally let herself *want...*

He exhaled hard and sat up, dragging a hand through his hair. That kiss had been a mistake... *his* mistake. He had lost control. And for a man like him, for a man with enemies, with a damaged name and a life built on the discipline of silence and strategy, *that* was dangerous.

He could not afford to want her because wanting led to needing, and needing led to weakness. And weakness always, *always* came at a cost.

***

The marble corridors of Westminster echoed beneath his boots, but Alaric felt the shift long before he entered the chamber. Something was not right.

It was in the way Lord Spencer's eyes flicked towards him, then quickly away. He recognised it in the way the younger peers grew suddenly engrossed in their papers as he passed. He noticed it in the unnatural hush that fell across benches where conversation had just moments before hummed like a swarm of bees.

He recognised the signs, for this was not a debate. This was a hunt.

Alaric kept his stride measured as he moved to his seat in the House of Lords with his expression carved from stone. He had faced worse in war, from ambushes and sabotage to the immeasurable weight of a dozen dying men in his arms. But this... this was *calculated*. And it was about to unfold in the cleanest, most civil manner treachery could take.

A page appeared before him with a quiet bow, handing over a sheaf of papers. Alaric took them without expression, unfolded the top sheet, and began to read.

Boundary irregularities... mismanagement of northern tenant lands... discrepancies in taxation ledgers...

The word *fraud* floated between paragraphs like a dagger left carelessly on a velvet cushion. The documents were vague, made deliberately so. Each sentence was crafted not to prove wrongdoing but to plant it like a seed that would eventually grow and blossom. Still, it was enough to invite questions, enough to suggest corruption without the burden of evidence, and finally, enough to let the whispers do their work.

He flipped through the stack slowly as rage simmered beneath his skin.

No names were signed, and no sources were cited. But the scent of his enemies clung to every line.

"Lord Ravensedge."

He looked up. Lord Huckleby stood nearby, white-haired, hunched with age but still possessed of a gaze as sharp as steel wire. He had served through three monarchs and a dozen scandals, but he had miraculously managed to do what few others had succeeded in doing before him: He had somehow kept his principles intact.

Alaric nodded once, gesturing him aside. They stepped away from the benches, behind one of the great columns, where a whisper could not carry so easily.

"They've come for me," Alaric said flatly, holding up the papers.

Huckleby took them, skimming the first page with a quiet hum.

"They always do, eventually," he murmured, "when they think you've bled enough to be manageable."

Alaric's mouth pulled tight. "It's orchestrated."

"I've no doubt." Huckleby folded the papers slowly. "The language is too carefully vague to be accidental. Slippery things. Designed to stick in a man's reputation without ever touching a law."

Alaric met his eyes. "Can it be stopped?"

"Truth?" The old man handed back the papers. "Not entirely. But you can hold the line. For now."

Alaric hated the performance of politics. He hated the idea of dancing for the same men who would gut him the moment he turned his back. But he'd seen enough battles to know that retreat was not always the wiser move.

"I'll need allies," he said quietly.

Huckleby gave him a long look. "Your name still holds weight with those who value merit over gossip. But they'll want something to believe in. You'll have to give them a reason."

Alaric exhaled through his nose. His jaw had been tight since dawn and hadn't once relaxed.

"I suppose a scandalously attractive wife is a start."

That earned him a dry chuckle.

"She'd do better than half the House," Huckleby said. "And with less posturing."

Alaric smiled back, patting the old man on the shoulder. "You are one of the rare ones, my lord. Don't ever change."

Upon those words, Alaric tucked the papers into his coat and stepped outside. Once back in his study at Ravensedge Hall, he found himself seated at his writing table with the stack of papers spread before him like a battlefield map. He read each claim again, slower this time.

It was all so carefully constructed, nothing solid enough to convict but just enough to cast doubt. Those were the sort of accusations that stuck not because they were true but because they were simply easy to believe.

"Misfiled boundaries on the northernmost edge of his holdings?" he read aloud to himself. He frowned. "That's land I haven't personally set foot on in over two years."

He continued reading. "Questionable rent increases on tenancies his steward had signed off without his hand... unexplained shifts in yield numbers from old tax rolls..."

Individually, each point could be dismissed. Together, they formed a picture of carelessness at best and deceit at worst. It wasn't a direct attack. It was erosion: a slow, steady attempt to rot his reputation from beneath.

He put the papers down, leaning back into his chair. Someone had planned this well in advance. This wasn't just some petty grudge or someone's idea of a joke. This was political, and exactly because it was political, it had to be calculated, timed with precision, and dropped like a blade the moment he'd begun to re-enter the public sphere.

He understood now that it had happened just after his first official appearance with his wife, just as murmurs were shifting and as his position had the hopes of stabilising.

The goal was obvious now. It was to tarnish him again before his marriage could restore him, to undercut his standing in the Lords, and to make him a liability to anyone considering support.

He let the breath leave his lungs slowly. Something assured him that whatever this was, it would not stop here. Whoever had orchestrated this wasn't looking for a single victory. No. They wanted to dismantle him piece by piece, to make his name so toxic that even loyalty would cost too much.

He stared at the fire, almost as if its light held the answers. But this was not a defeat. It was a declaration of war.

They thought him ruined. They thought him disgraced and bleeding, breathing his last breath. But they'd miscalculated because Alaric Vale knew how to survive an ambush, and more importantly, he knew how to return fire.

He rose from his chair with his hands curling at his sides. This was only the beginning. And someone, somewhere, had just made the grave mistake of forgetting that he'd once been a man who led charges through the hell of blood and smoke.

Chapter Eighteen

"I made a mistake," Catharine said quietly, her gaze fixed on the untouched tea in her saucer.

Eliza blinked, head tilting just slightly. "That doesn't sound like you."

They sat alone in the drawing room with the late afternoon sun catching the lace at the windows and dust motes dancing in the stillness. The hearth was warm, the atmosphere peaceful, but the tightness in Catharine's chest made everything feel too loud.

"I let something happen again," she said, still not looking at her sister. "With Alaric."

Eliza didn't interrupt.

"I don't regret it," Catharine added. "I mean… I don't know if I do…"

That was the crux of it. In fact, she hadn't meant to say anything to her sister. Vulnerability was not her currency. She had always been the poised one, the reliable one. She was the sister who watched from the edge of the ballroom rather than stepping onto it. But the silence between her and Alaric these past days had twisted something inside her she could no longer ignore.

"I let myself believe," she said, voice low, "that maybe he wanted more than duty, that maybe what happened between us meant something. We kissed at the ball a few days ago, and it is all the same as before. We are like strangers in this house."

"Did you try to seduce him?" Eliza asked curiously.

"I tried to make him jealous," Catharine admitted.

"Ah, yes, at the ball." Eliza nodded. "I would say you were rather successful at it."

Catharine frowned. "I don't know if I managed to succeed in anything. I just made him angry... furious, even. Then..."

"Yes, I know what happened," Eliza reminded her gently. "I think all of the ton knows what happened, but that doesn't matter now. You got him where you wanted him to be: mesmerised by you. Wasn't that what you wished for?"

Catharine inhaled deeply. "I don't know. I don't want to push him or trick him into anything. I just want him to be honest with me, to tell me how he truly feels about all of this. Instead, I feel like we're playing games of hot and cold."

Eliza set her tea down with a soft click and leaned forward with her elbows on her knees and her hands clasped. "Catharine... you've always been careful, always in control. But men like Alaric don't respond to logic. They respond to instinct, to need."

Catharine's brow arched faintly. "You're suggesting I make my husband *need* me?"

"I'm suggesting," Eliza said, her voice low and amused, "that you make him *need* to chase you."

"But that means I chase him first, and I don't chase."

"You wouldn't have to. You'd only have to... remind him what he's missing."

A silence passed between them as Catharine considered that.

Eliza smiled, but there was steel beneath it. "This isn't about lowering yourself. It's about shifting the balance. If he's going to act like what happened meant nothing, then fine. Let him stew in it. But you, my dear sister, are going to be unforgettable, just like you were at the ball last time."

"But I can't possibly wear such a gown at home," Catharine gasped in mock horror.

"Why not?" Eliza replied playfully. "You can even be nude at home. Who's to stop you?"

"Subtle," Catharine murmured, suppressing a chuckle.

"Devastating," Eliza corrected.

Another moment of silence passed before Catharine reached for her long-cold tea, still lost in thought. She had spent so long guarding herself against hurt, against shame, that she'd forgotten what it meant to want and to be wanted in return. But Alaric had kissed her like a man unravelling, and no matter what he'd said after, she hadn't imagined that.

She wouldn't beg for his attention. But she *could* shift the ground beneath his feet, just like she had done at the ball. So that night, Catharine dressed with intent. She opted for no corset, no lace, and no jewels. The only thing she did choose was silk: soft, pale, and perilously delicate.

The robe fell like water over her frame, tied loosely at the waist, the neckline gaping just enough to suggest carelessness rather than design. But every detail was chosen, and every brush of fabric against her skin was strategic.

For this was not seduction. It was a shift in power.

She moved through their shared spaces with quiet ease, a picture of elegant distraction. She lit a candle in the library with slow, unhurried fingers, while he was there, focused on a book. She paused by the decanter on the sideboard and poured a glass of wine she didn't plan on drinking. She made sure her posture was graceful but relaxed, as though she had forgotten anyone might be looking.

She felt him before she saw him, standing somewhere beyond the edge of the firelight. His presence always charged the room, even when he said nothing. Or perhaps especially then. But Catharine didn't look at him.

Instead, she let her gaze linger on the fire, her fingers wrapped loosely around the wine glass, her other hand adjusting the robe at her shoulder, letting it slip just slightly before catching it again. It was a calculated motion, done as though by accident.

Let him wonder if it was for him.

Despite her initial plans, she took a slow sip of the wine, allowing it to gently wash over her senses. Her desire was emblazoned, but she kept it under control, for she wanted *him* out of control, not herself. Her eyes flicked towards the open book abandoned on the writing table, then she turned away as if she wasn't even aware of his existence.

Only then did she allow herself to glance at him, just briefly and only once as she passed through the library doors and into the hall with the hem of her robe brushing against the floor in her wake. Then, suddenly, his hand closed around her wrist. It was not hard, but it was firm.

She stopped, turning to him. They were now inches apart, with her eyes questioning him. His gaze raked down the length of her, slow and merciless, stopping at the faint dip in her collarbone where the silk had slipped just slightly, then climbing back to her face. When he spoke, his voice was low and dark, nestled somewhere between a warning and something far more dangerous.

"I know what you're trying to do."

Her brow arched, calm as marble. "Do you?"

"You're not ready for it," he said, the words sharp as flint. "So whatever game you're playing... stop."

She held his stare, unblinking.

"My lord," she said coolly, "I haven't the faintest idea what you're talking about."

The faintest flicker crossed his face. Was it frustration? Or something darker, more unsettled? His grip loosened, though he didn't step back. She slipped her wrist from his hand slowly without flinching. Then, as if nothing had happened, she turned and walked away, listening to the sound of the silk whispering at her heels.

He didn't follow. She didn't think he would dare. But she felt his gaze burning down her spine with every step she took. Knowing he couldn't see her, she smiled.

That night, she lay in her bed with her back pressed to the wall and the sheets cool against her burning skin. The moonlight reached only partway across the room, leaving shadows curled at the corners. Her eyes stayed wide open in the dark. She couldn't sleep, not when the memory of his hand around her waist lingered in her mind.

She had walked away like it didn't touch her, like *he* didn't touch her. But now, alone with nothing but her own breath and the ache behind her ribs, she admitted what she hadn't let show. She *had* started something, and she didn't know how to stop it. In fact, she didn't even know if she wanted to stop it.

She had never felt like this before. There had been affection with her previous suitors, with the viscount who'd left her three days before their wedding. There had been a kind of gentleness. But never this raw, almost cruel magnetism that pulled at something buried so deep inside her she barely recognised it as hers.

She *wanted* Alaric.

Not just his hands or his mouth, though God knew those haunted her mind and body now. No, she wanted something else, something far worse and far more dangerous. She wanted to know what lived behind those dark eyes when he wasn't pushing her away. She wanted to hear what truth he carried when he wasn't speaking like war was still breathing down his neck. She wanted honesty, brutal if it had to be, even if it tore something in her.

If this, whatever *this* was, meant nothing to him, she wanted him to say so. If kissing her had been a mistake, she wanted to hear him admit it. If the pleasure he gave her was born only of frustration or proximity or temporary madness, she needed to know.

Because heartbreak, she could survive. But false hope? That was the more dangerous cruelty.

Catharine's eyes drifted shut, but sleep still didn't come.

Strangely enough, she didn't fear ruin anymore. But she did fear wanting a man who wouldn't let himself want her back. And if he did...

She feared what would happen if he ever said so out loud.

Chapter Nineteen

"He wants an alliance?" Alaric's voice was flat, the words edged with contempt. "Blackmoor doesn't ally; he acquires other people and their assets."

The study door had been locked an hour ago, and a decanter of brandy stood half-drained on the sideboard. None of the three men had touched their breakfast. Rhys Ashbourne was seated in his usual uncompromising silence with his fingers steepled beneath his chin and his expression carved from granite. Across from him, Dorian Gainsworth lounged with deceptive ease in an armchair, cravat askew and one boot propped on the opposite knee.

"He approached me directly," Rhys said at last. "He suggested that if I were willing to reconsider my position on several proposed land tariffs, his support in upcoming matters could be, and I quote: *mutually beneficial.*"

Alaric exhaled through his nose. "Which means he thinks you're wavering."

Rhys' mouth curved slightly. Whether that was in amusement or warning was hard to tell. "Which means he's testing the water to see how deep the rot goes."

Dorian snorted and threw back a swallow of brandy. "If Blackmoor's involved, there's more rot than Parliament has chairs for. And if he's sniffing around you, he's already laid his traps elsewhere."

Alaric's jaw tightened.

It was the same name that had surfaced too many times in recent weeks. Blackmoor had always kept himself half in shadow, which meant well-connected, well-funded, and just honourable enough to avoid scandal while helping create it for others.

Now he was circling, and he was doing so too close.

"Do you think he's behind the smear campaign?" Alaric asked.

Dorian's expression darkened. "I'd bet my title on it. The language in those documents? That sort of half-truth, half-poison structure? It's how he operates, just enough doubt to make a man reek of guilt without ever proving a thing."

Rhys rose and walked to the window, his back stiff with thought.

"I can reach out to Lord Creighton," he said. "He used to serve on the same estate board as Blackmoor. If anyone knows which clerks or stewards could be manipulated, it would be him."

Alaric nodded once. "We need proof. Something tangible."

"And when we have it?" Dorian asked, voice casual but eyes gleaming.

"Then we make it public," Alaric said. "Let the same mouths that whispered against me bite down on something real."

Rhys turned from the window. "This won't be clean."

"I'm not expecting clean," Alaric muttered. "I'm expecting *war*."

There was a pause. Then Dorian tipped his glass in a mock-toast. "Well. At least we're all finally speaking the same language."

Just as Alaric was about to say that it was too early for a toast, the door burst open without so much as a knock.

"Forgive the intrusion," came Isadora's breezy voice, "but we have a problem involving hooves and impatience."

Alaric looked up sharply, already bracing. Isadora strode in with the ease of someone who had never once cared for decorum. Behind her, Catharine followed as the perfect counterpoint, being elegant, composed, and unreadable. She wore a deep green riding habit that clung at the waist and flared at the hip, her dark hair pulled into a sleek knot. The sight of her hit him with an absurd, almost violent clarity.

"I'm not sure what sort of beasts you keep stabled here," Isadora went on, hands on her hips, "but one of the geldings has thrown a shoe. And I have no intention of circling the lake on that lumbering old mare from the back pasture. So I propose a trade."

Alaric arched a brow. "You intend to borrow *my* horse?"

"No," Isadora said sweetly. "Catharine does. I even have a special outfit for her to ride astride, so she is all set."

Alaric glanced towards his wife. Catharine met his gaze steadily. Her lips parted as if she might object, but she didn't. Her expression remained cool, even as something flickered in the depths of her eyes.

He considered it, for his stallion was no idle creature. He was powerful, proud, temperamental. He tolerated only experienced riders, and even then, he tested them. He could throw a grown man with a flick of his neck if given half an excuse.

"She can handle him," Isadora added as mischief curled in her voice. "Don't let the hairpins and manners fool you."

Alaric didn't move for a moment.

"She's not a girl, Izza," he said slowly. "And that horse isn't a pony to trot around a rose garden."

"I'm aware," Catharine said. Her voice was calm, but the steel in it was unmistakable. "I can manage him."

The certainty in her tone did something to him, something unexpected and unwanted.

He nodded just once. "Very well."

Isadora grinned, rushing over to him to give him a peck on the cheek, which was something he didn't like, and she knew it. "Perfect. We'll be back before luncheon."

Alaric watched as they turned and swept back out the door, a flurry of feminine confidence and wind-chilled silk. The study's silence settled again in their wake, but the atmosphere had changed, having been fractured slightly by the scent of Catharine's perfume and the aftershock of her quiet challenge.

Dorian let out a low whistle. "Brave woman. Or mad."

Alaric wasn't sure if he meant Izza or Catharine. Not that it mattered. He turned back towards the window. Outside, two figures crossed the gravel towards the stables. One was laughing, the other was silent, her posture straight as a blade.

She'd ride the devil if it meant proving a point, he thought to himself.

And God help him, he couldn't decide if he was worried or impressed.

With the women gone, the men returned to the map spread across the writing table. Rhys was pacing near the hearth while Dorian pored over names with a scowl. About half an hour had elapsed when Alaric leaned over the papers, only to hear a sound tear through the morning air like a blade.

A scream. It was high, sharp, and unmistakably *hers.*

Everything in him stilled for half a second, just long enough for his heart to miss its beat. Then he was moving. The study door slammed behind him. He took the steps two at a time, his boots pounding down the hall, across the stone foyer, through the arch to the eastern terrace. Someone shouted behind him, Dorian maybe, but he didn't hear.

The courtyard flashed past. The stables loomed ahead. And then, there she was, lying on the edge of the gravel path near the far slope. Catharine's body was still, and her riding coat twisted with one glove torn. The sight of her made his blood run cold.

Alaric dropped to his knees beside her. "Catharine?"

Her eyes fluttered open. Her lips parted in a shaky breath, but no words flowed.

"I'm here," he said, one hand on her face, the other cradling the back of her head, trying not to tremble. "You're all right. You're all right, I've got you."

She winced. "The horse—"

"Forget the damn horse."

His gaze swept over her, assessing. There was blood on her palm and dirt on her cheek. One boot was twisted... her ankle. Her shoulder, too, maybe. She was breathing, talking, conscious... but clearly in pain.

"Send for Doctor Jennings," he told one of the servant girls, who immediately rushed back to the house, following his order.

As Alaric took off his coat in an effort to pick Catharine up into his arms, he noticed the stallion a few paces away. The animal was nervous but not wild. His eyes landed on the saddle as one of the stablehands reached for the reins. At first glance, everything looked intact.

But then he saw it. The girth strap was snapped clean through. It wasn't frayed. It wasn't worn out. It was *cut* so neatly that it would be nearly invisible unless one knew where to look.

"I'll be right back," he whispered to Catharine, then went to the horse and confirmed his suspicions with a single glance.

This wasn't an accident. This wasn't some foolish, almost tragic mistake by a stable boy or a skittish mount on uneven ground. Someone had done this... deliberately, which meant that same someone had meant to injure him, and Catharine had paid the price.

He shuddered at the thought of what might have been. He immediately returned to her.

"Don't move," he urged. He slid one arm beneath her knees, the other beneath her back, and lifted her with a care that felt more like desperation. She gave a low, strangled cry but clutched at him for safety.

"I'm sorry," she whispered, catching him completely off guard.

He looked down at her sharply. "Don't you dare apologise."

Her eyes met his. "I should've—"

"No," he snapped, his voice on the verge of breaking. "Just— no."

His grip on her tightened. Catharine shifted against his chest with a faint gasp, and his fury dissolved, just for a breath, beneath the rise of sickening guilt.

He said nothing to her. He adjusted her gently in his arms and carried her across the gravel back into the house. Each stride was measured and controlled. But inside, the rage was climbing like a storm up his spine.

She made no sound now. Her cheek rested against his shoulder, and her breathing was shallow but even. She was trying not to show pain, as always. She was trying not to be a burden. That thought alone nearly undid him.

They passed the front hall, the shocked staff parting wordlessly. Izza hovered at the edge of the stairs, pale but composed, already barking orders to the butler behind her.

"Fetch warm water. Towels. Some whiskey for the pain," he told them.

"I'll see to it," Isadora replied at once. "Is she—"

"Later," he said. It wasn't cold, but it *was* final.

He took her to their chamber, not the one she used when keeping distance between them, but theirs, the same one he'd had prepared for her comfort when they'd first arrived at Ravensedge. The door was already open, the bed freshly turned. He laid her down with care, brushing the hair from her temple.

"Don't sleep yet," he said quietly.

Her eyes fluttered. "I'm not."

"Good," he murmured. "Stay awake a little longer."

She searched his face for something, but he didn't know what. Still, whatever that was, he couldn't give it, not while his blood still burned with the knowledge of how close she'd come to breaking because of him.

He sat beside her until the physician arrived, saying nothing, while the broken strap burned into his memory.

Whoever had done this had made one mistake. They'd hurt her to get to him.

And now he would find them, and he would destroy them.

Chapter Twenty

"Margaret, I promise I'm not dying," Catharine said dryly, "though the way you're attacking that pillow suggests you'd like to smother me gently just in case."

"I'm fluffing, not smothering," Margaret replied with tragic intensity, adjusting the down-stuffed cushion for the fifth time. "You need support. And warmth. And Eliza, do we have more blankets?"

Eliza, already by the hearth and halfway through a lecture to the maid about lavender compresses, didn't even look up. "She doesn't need more blankets. She needs to breathe, Maggie."

"I'm breathing just fine," Catharine muttered, eyeing the ever-growing pile of shawls, cushions, and embroidered nonsense now overtaking the chaise.

It had been two days, and the pain in her ankle had dulled to a persistent throb. In fact, it was a reminder of the fall, of the horse, and lastly, of the man who'd carried her inside with silent fury and a jaw so tight she'd thought it might crack. What she hadn't expected was the parade of chaos that had followed her injury.

Margaret had arrived first, wide-eyed and blotchy-cheeked, as if Catharine had been dragged from a shipwreck rather than pitched from a saddle. She'd burst into the room trailing half a dozen concerns and two unmatched gloves. Then came Eliza, calm and commanding as always, issuing unnecessary orders in the voice of a duchess accustomed to handling everything from court scandals to broken teacups.

"I don't understand why you were even on his horse," Margaret said now, smoothing her skirts and glancing towards the door with a touch too much curiosity. "That dreadful beast looked like something out of one of Papa's hunting prints."

"He's not dreadful," Catharine replied, shifting slightly and stifling a wince. "Just... misunderstood. I do hope to try and ride him again."

Margaret blinked. "Catharine, the horse tried to kill you."

"Margaret." Eliza's tone warned of older-sister impatience. "Whatever happened, I'm certain it wasn't the horse's fault."

"Well, it certainly wasn't Catharine's," Margaret said loyally, reaching to pat her hand. "She's always ridden beautifully. You remember the year she outraced Lord Ellesmere's son and ruined his pride for a fortnight?"

Catharine gave a small, fond huff. "He still glares at me in ballrooms."

"Serves him right," Eliza murmured, folding her arms. "But let's not pretend this was a harmless fall. You must rest now, my dear."

Rhys arrived next with all the sisters still present. He entered without ceremony.

"You should've ridden something with fewer teeth," he muttered, coming to stand beside Eliza.

"He doesn't have teeth," Catharine said, managing a faint smile. "He has... opinions."

Rhys grunted with his arms crossed. But his eyes swept over her with the kind of intensity that betrayed far more concern than he would ever admit aloud.

"She'll recover," Eliza assured him, patting his arm. "Physically, at least. Whether she ever agrees to ride again is another matter."

"Don't be ridiculous," Catharine said. "I'll ride again the moment I can walk without limping."

That earned a small flicker of amusement from Rhys before he leaned in, brushing his lips against the top of her head, which was a rare, unspoken offering. Then, without another word, he turned and stalked out again.

Margaret blinked. "Did he just... was that affection?"

Eliza smirked. "He'll deny it by supper."

The door flew open once more.

"Oh, for heaven's sake," came Isadora's voice, pitched high with fury. "Look at this fire. It's practically a candle. And why does the tea taste like boiled linens?"

"Isadora," Catharine said with a weary sigh, "I'm fine, truly."

"No, you're not!" Isadora turned to the nearest maid. "Bring more tea. No, bring *better* tea. Bring something that doesn't smell like regret."

Catharine tried not to laugh. It hurt to move too much.

"Izza," she said carefully, "I appreciate the drama. But if you fluff one more pillow, I may expire just to spite you."

Isadora froze, hand halfway to another cushion. "Fine," she muttered. "I'll go scream into the drapes."

She didn't, of course. She sat beside Margaret instead, dabbing at her cheeks with an entirely unnecessary lace handkerchief. The chaos was just beginning to calm when another knock on the door revealed Lord Dorian Gainsworth.

"Ah," he said grandly, striding in with a bouquet of lavender and a ridiculous smirk. "I was told there was a fallen lady in distress. Imagine my disappointment to find you merely resting." He leaned in to offer the flowers. "For your convalescence."

"Are those from the garden?" Isadora gasped.

"Freshly stolen," he agreed.

Catharina couldn't resist chuckling. "Thank you. Your concern is touching."

Dorian smirked and turned to take a seat, except he misjudged the low table behind him. With a loud crash, his boot caught the edge, toppling it and the tea tray in one spectacular clang of porcelain and startled gasps.

Isadora was on her feet in an instant. "You absolute menace!"

"Oh, please," Dorian said, brushing off his sleeve. "It was an attack of grief. My limbs betrayed me."

"You've ruined the carpet!"

"I improved it. And perhaps it's your presence making me clumsy."

"Oh, do not start with me, Gainsworth."

Catharine lay back against the cushions, watching the two of them like a badly choreographed play. Their bickering had become its own form of comfort.

Something warm curled in her chest beneath the noise, the endless overlapping voices, the well-meaning panic. It wasn't the tea. It wasn't even the absurd scent of lavender now wafting from Gainsworth's pilfered bouquet. It was *them,* all of them.

It was Margaret folding and refolding the corner of the blanket while pretending not to cry. It was Eliza issuing instructions like a general, though no one quite needed them.

It was Izza threatening to storm the stables and interrogate the stablehands herself. It was even Gainsworth, ridiculous and smug and somehow perfectly in place among the chaos. And it was also Rhys, who was blunt, grim, and silent in his affection, the kind of man who would set the world aflame and claim it was just weather if it meant protecting someone he loved.

A strange comfort settled inside her like a hush beneath the din. Perhaps she mattered more than she thought. Perhaps she mattered not just as a daughter, or a sister, or a name on the marriage roll of a marquess, but as herself. The thought unnerved her almost as much as it soothed.

"I think," she said slowly, "I might survive this ordeal after all."

"Oh, thank God," Margaret exhaled, collapsing into a chair.

"You never had a flair for drama," Eliza teased. "It suits you."

"I've never fallen off a horse in my life," Catharine murmured. "I honestly don't know what's more unsettling: the fall or the fact I didn't see it coming."

Isadora stepped forward, her expression gentler now, though still edged with exasperation. "No one sees it coming, my dear. That's what falling *is*. Whether it's a horse or... something else entirely."

Her gaze lingered. Her body ached. But her heart ached, too, in a way she didn't quite understand. She let her gaze drift towards the door, not expecting him or needing him.

But wondering if maybe, just maybe, he'd come anyway.

***

When everyone finally left, the room fell into a hush so complete it felt almost unreal. Catharine hadn't noticed how loud they'd been until the silence settled, like velvet drawn over her senses.

She shifted slightly, adjusting the blanket over her legs. And then she heard it: the scrape of a chair being pulled closer.

He hadn't said a word since the others left. He hadn't announced his intention to stay. But there he was, rolling up his sleeves at the forearm with calm precision, exposing strong wrists, the kind shaped by years of command, not ease. His coat was already discarded somewhere. She hadn't seen when.

He crouched at the edge of the chaise, his knees brushing the rug, and reached for her injured ankle.

"You don't need to—" she began shyly.

"I know," he said simply.

But his hands were already there, warm and steady. His fingers moved with a strange kind of reverence, gathering her foot gently, adjusting the pillow beneath her calf. Then, slowly, he began to press his thumbs into the arch of her foot, tracing slow, deliberate circles. She felt his touch everywhere, not just in the delicate bones of her ankle but behind her knees, at the base of her spine, beneath her skin.

He worked in silence, the pads of his thumbs finding the places where ache lingered. He didn't speak or look up. But every motion was careful, attentive, almost... intimate. And it was too much after all those days of cold distance, of tight glances and silence sharp enough to wound.

His thumb drifted along the bone of her ankle. She looked down at him then, and he finally looked up at her. Her breath caught as his hand travelled upward with cautious purpose, his fingers feeling her bare skin. The warmth of his palm lingered there. It was too reverent to be improper and too steady to be ignored. His hand stilled just below her knee.

"I... I thought I lost you," Alaric said, his voice rough as gravel.

She blinked, startled by the rawness of it, by the vulnerability in his voice. It was as if every carefully locked door inside him had swung open at once. This made her braver than she had ever been.

"Then stop," she whispered. "Stop torturing me."

His brows knit as if he didn't understand. She had to explain, even at the price of losing him.

She sat forward slightly, ignoring the dull throb in her ankle, ignoring everything but him. "You kiss me like it means something. You look at me like I'm yours. And then you pull away like it never happened. You're driving me mad."

All he had at first was silence, thick and pulsing. Then his voice flooded her, low and certain.

"I can't do it anymore."

She stilled.

"I told myself I wouldn't care. That this was duty, nothing more. That keeping distance was a strength. But it's not. It's cowardice." His jaw tensed. "Because I've already fallen, Catharine. And I can't protect myself from you."

The world stopped spinning. Her breath caught. For a heartbeat, neither of them moved.

Then she reached for him slowly, carefully, fingers brushing the edge of his jaw. He met her halfway, but this kiss was nothing like the others. There were no sharp edges, no hunger disguised as anger. It was slow and almost devastating in its tenderness.

His hands framed her face. Her fingers slid into his hair. When they parted, her forehead rested against his, and their hearts were racing in rhythm.

"I don't know how to be loved," she whispered, still afraid of what all of this might mean.

His thumb brushed her cheek.

"Then we'll learn together."

Chapter Twenty-One

Alaric stirred as the early light breached the heavy damask curtains, stretching its long fingers across the chamber walls. He hadn't meant to fall asleep, and certainly not like this. Yet here he was, still tangled with *her.*

His arm lay draped across Catharine's waist. Her back was to him, her spine resembling a graceful line that curved into the warm shelter of his chest. The scent of her hair lingered throughout the night. He already knew it well: lavender and something faintly citrusy, like bergamot tea. It was still clinging to the linen and invading his lungs with every inhale.

She had not moved through the night, and neither had he.

Alaric blinked against the pale morning light. For the first time in what felt like years, his mind was not instantly pulled into memory. There was no gunfire, no screams, no betrayal. There was just blissful silence, and in the very centre of it, *her.* The even rhythm of her breath steadied something in him he had never thought would steady again.

For Alaric Vale was not a man given to comfort. The war had bled softness out of him, and politics had trampled the rest. But her warmth against his side, the delicate bones of her wrist nestled in his palm... this was something else, a tenderness he didn't recognise and almost didn't trust.

He could still hear the echo of her fall, the sheer terror of the aftermath. He had never moved so fast in his life, gathering her into his arms before she had even registered the pain. And then she had clung to him not out of propriety or from calculation but instinct.

Now in the quiet grey light, she stirred. It was just the smallest shift of her shoulder. Then a breath caught at the base of her throat, but she slowly calmed once more, and that was exactly when a knock on the door came without warning.

He recognised it immediately. It was too quick for servants and too familiar for courtesy. Before he could get up and open the door himself, it opened with deliberate slowness, and Isadora peered through it. She stood there in the doorway, still wrapped in her silk morning robe with an absurd-looking peacock embroidered across the front like some private jest. She was holding a teacup with both hands now as steam coiled past her face.

She froze the moment she took in the room. Her gaze rested specifically on the tangled sheets and Catharine, who was still asleep, still curled like a question he didn't know how to answer. Then Isadora smiled. It was not a smirk exactly but rather something delighted, almost triumphant.

"I would say forgive the intrusion," she whispered, her eyes dancing with amusement, "but I rather think I've walked into the most promising development this household has seen in years."

Alaric gave her a withering look and rose from the bed, grabbing the dressing robe slung nearby.

"She's sleeping," he said under his breath.

"I noticed," Isadora replied, mock-solemn. "And for once, so were you. Miracles abound."

He scowled, but she only held up one hand, placating her.

"Don't worry. I won't wake your lady. Though I'm tempted to draw her a bath and fetch her slippers myself. The poor thing's earned it."

Alaric crossed the room, blocking her view out of sheer instinct. "Did you come for a reason or only to rattle my temper?"

Isadora stepped back into the hall, grinning. "Both, naturally. But also, there's an envelope waiting in your study, marked urgent. It arrived by courier not half an hour ago."

Something in her tone shifted then. The levity drained just a fraction.

Alaric nodded once tightly. "Thank you."

"I'll see that breakfast is kept warm."

She offered him one last meaningful glance, which was half conspirator, half sister-in-arms, and then eased the door shut without another word.

He turned back, just for a moment. Catharine had shifted slightly, turning around with her hand resting now on the place where his body had been. Her brow furrowed in sleep, as if some part of her had already registered his absence. He hesitated, but then he forced himself to move.

About five minutes later, he was in his study, and it was exactly as he had left it the night before, with a stack of correspondence on the writing table in a familiar, tedious order, except for the new envelope. It sat apart from the rest with its thick, cream paper and Ashbourne's seal.

The letter was brief but heavy with implication. Alaric sat back in his chair, surveying his friend's unmistakable hand, for it was sharp, slanted, and economical, just like the man himself. There were no superfluous turns of phrase, just facts, laid out like a general dispatch.

A witness has come forward. Come see me urgently.

Alaric read the line again, then again. The air in the study seemed to thicken. He exhaled once, slowly, willing his pulse to steady. His scar itched faintly, as it always did when he was under pressure. He didn't reach for it.

There was no signature. Ashbourne never signed his letters. If one were intercepted, there would be nothing to tie the contents back to him. Not that anyone with sense wouldn't recognise the voice in those lines.

Now, finally, there was a real move, a real witness... proof, even.

Alaric leaned forward, bracing his elbows on the edge of the desk, one hand pressed over the letter, the other clenched into a fist. The truth had become a weight he carried quietly, privately. He had told himself he no longer needed vindication, that survival was enough.

But now...?

A man could live with ruin. He had done it for years.

But justice for a loved one?

That was a different kind of hunger.

The crack of the hearth settling made him look up. Across the room, the flames had guttered low. He noticed that Catharine's gloves still lay where she'd left them, as if in her absence, she was still bracing for battle.

His jaw flexed. She had risked everything by marrying him. She had chosen him not because she believed in him but because she believed in herself. And he'd given her no reason, yet, to do otherwise.

He reached for the gloves. Held them a moment in his scarred hand. Then he stood.

He had places to go and people to see.

***

The stableyard behind the dilapidated coaching inn stank of old hay, sweat, and mildew. Alaric adjusted his coat, the wool damp from fog, and glanced once at Ashbourne, who stood just behind him, silent as always. His gloved hands were folded behind his back, and his gaze was fixed on the stable door like a hawk waiting for a twitch in the grass.

They knew that the stableman, Thomas Richards, was still inside.

Alaric exhaled through his nose. Then he stepped forward and pushed the door open. Inside, the air was thick with the scent of wet straw and horse musk. A single lantern burned low on a hook. And there, seated on an overturned feed barrel, head bowed and shoulders hunched like a man sentenced, sat Thomas.

He was younger than Alaric expected, barely thirty, if that. His cap lay crumpled in his hands, and his eyes seemed red and raw. Alaric assumed that he had been drinking, but as they approached him, there was no stink of spirits about him.

The moment he looked up and saw them, his face crumpled further.

"I knew you'd come lookin' for me," he said, his voice cutting off.

Alaric said nothing. He just shut the door behind them. Ashbourne moved to lean against a post, the picture of composed menace.

"You tampered with Lady Vale's saddle," Alaric informed him, surprising even himself how calm he was. That was good.

That would allow for a better punishment of the man who had almost taken Catharine from him. "Seven days ago."

Thomas nodded, then shook his head, as if unsure which gesture was true. "I... I did. A little cut, where it wouldn't show. I didn't know she'd be the one to fall. I just... he said it'd be harmless. Just enough to frighten you."

Alaric knew well that it was an attempt at his own life. But whoever had ordered it had made a grave mistake and targeted Catharine instead.

"'He,'" Rhys repeated softly, his voice like glass against stone. "Who is this *he*?"

Thomas' lip trembled. He rubbed a sleeve across his face and muttered something, low and garbled.

Alaric stepped forward. "Speak clearly."

The man broke, his voice cracking. "Lord Blackmoor. I didn't know his name at first, only that he came through a man, high coat, southern accent, riding gloves with pearl buttons. He paid me in coin and said more would come if I did as told."

"Did he threaten you?" Ashbourne asked for more clarification.

Alaric could feel his rage pounding through the surface of his skin. He wanted to break this man's neck for what he had done, mistake or not. But the man's pitiful expression and voice, which was already on the verge of breaking without having suffered any physical blowout, made Alaric halt in his intentions.

"No, my lord," the man stuttered. "He knew of my family's condition... He just promised... enough for my wife's medicine, for the baby." He covered his face then. "God help me, I didn't think... I didn't know she'd fall hard. She's a *lady*, and I... I didn't mean—"

Alaric watched the man weep as guilt bloomed out of him like rot. He believed him. The cut on the saddle had been clean and calculated. It was not the work of a man who wanted blood, just one who was desperate enough to accept money for an immoral deed.

It was a man who was desperate as well as used by none other than Lord Blackmoor.

The name curdled in Alaric's gut. Ashbourne didn't move. He didn't blink. But Alaric saw the shift in his posture as well.

He had always suspected Blackmoor. Alaric knew of the way he'd slithered around Parliament, muttering about his own unfitness, laughing too easily when Catharine's name was raised in scandal.

Still, proof mattered, and now they had it.

Alaric crouched before the man. "You'll give a statement," he instructed him. "Anonymous, if it must be. But you'll write what you did, and who paid you to do it."

Thomas nodded without hesitation.

"I'll see to it your family gets that medicine," Alaric added. "But if you disappear before the ink is dry, I will find you. Understood?"

The stableman nodded once again, pale and shaking.

That was when Ashbourne turned towards the door. "Come, Ravensedge. We have what we came for."

As they stepped back into the mist, the sun was just beginning to burn through the grey. Ashbourne walked in silence by his friend's side, as he adjusted the leather of his gloves with slow, meticulous care, akin to a man sharpening a blade he might soon put to use.

Alaric felt his jaw tighten even more. "He's after more than my seat."

Ashbourne didn't look over. "Naturally."

They walked a few more paces in silence.

"Why now?" Alaric asked. "He's hated me for years. But he waited until Catharine?"

Rhys made a faint sound in his throat, which was part scoff, part agreement.

"I assume she has made you palatable again," he explained. "After the war, after the scandal... you were unofficially exiled from the ton. You were damaged goods. Parliament whispered, clubs laughed, and half the lords took bets on how long it would take for you to drink yourself into irrelevance."

Alaric gave a humourless smile. "Charming."

Ashbourne went on, undeterred. "Then you married her. Catharine Fairbourne, who is, by all accounts, cold, brilliant, and untouchable. The one who was meant to marry up, not down. The papers hated it, of course. But society? Society began to... wonder."

Alaric felt the truth of it settle in his bones. "You think Blackmoor fears a resurgence."

Ashbourne finally looked at him then with eyes sharp beneath his dark lashes. "I think he fears competition."

Alaric frowned. "He's never cared about real policy. He speaks to hear his own voice."

"Yes," Ashbourne said dryly. "And that voice is growing louder. The merchant class loves him. He's promising reform without substance, popularity without risk. And you?" He smiled, thin and cold. "You were the one man who could call him out on the floor without losing the room."

Alaric exhaled slowly. "So he tried to provoke me. Through her."

Ashbourne nodded once. "Make you look like a brute, a failure. Let your temper do the rest."

"He wanted me to crack."

"More than that," Ashbourne added, his tone quiet now. "He wanted *her* to doubt you, probably even to leave you. If Catharine had ended the marriage publicly, it would've been over. Your redemption, your alliances, your marriage, and finally, your legacy."

Alaric looked away, the ache in his chest sharp and sudden. She hadn't left, even when she had every reason to. Instead, she had stood beside him after the fall. He had no right to that kind of loyalty, but he had it.

And now? He would earn it.

"I'll start leaking Blackmoor's name in the right corners, carefully. No accusations, just questions, enough to plant doubt," Alaric informed him.

They reached the horses, waiting quietly in the mist.

Alaric paused before mounting. "He targeted my wife."

Ashbourne's eyes flicked to him. "I know."

"I'll see him ruined."

Ashbourne smiled faintly. "Now *that* sounds like the Ravensedge I've been told about."

They rode in silence for a long time after that. Behind them, somewhere in the shadows of the stable, a frightened man was thinking of the words to write down his truth in ink.

War, as Alaric knew, had many forms.

And this one would be his to win, no matter what.

Chapter Twenty-Two

Catharine woke slowly, as though rising from the depths of a fevered dream. Warmth still clung to her skin, and the scent of him still lingered. Her hand drifted out beneath the coverlet, searching instinctively... but there was nothing. The space beside her was cool and empty.

For a long moment, she lay there, staring at the pale light on the ceiling. The hearth had gone cold. The silence of the room pressed in like snow.

He is gone.

Her throat tightened, but she forced herself to sit upright. The shift of the bedsheets sounded loud in the stillness.

So this is it.

She swung her legs over the edge of the bed and placed her feet on the rug. The cold of the floorboards seeped through. Her robe hung neatly from the chair by the hearth. He hadn't even disturbed it.

He'd simply left without a word, without a note, without a single glance back, as though nothing had happened.

Her chest, just like her ankle, ached. Fortunately, it was not a sharp pain but dull and low, like an old wound pressed too hard. She drew the robe around herself with precise fingers, with every movement calm and controlled. She was immaculate, as always, as a bitter certainty settled in her chest.

Of course, it didn't mean anything to him.

It was nothing but a shared night born out of pity and proximity, a tender moment which she had mistaken for something more. She should have known better. He was a soldier, trained in discipline and detachment. And she was a Fairbourne, trained in nothing so dangerous as hope.

Still, she had let herself drift, if only for just a moment, just long enough to forget the rules she herself had written to prevent this very exact thing from happening. And now she would pay the price.

Catharine stood and slowly walked to the window. The dull throbbing in her ankle was present, but she needed to move, so she kept stabilizing herself against the furniture, taking it one step at a time.

Morning had laid a weak sun across the moors, all pale gold and grey clouds. The estate beyond lay quiet and utterly serene. But she could feel the shift beneath it, like a thread pulled too tight, threatening to snap. She wrapped her arms around herself and exhaled slowly.

No more foolishness.

By the time her maid had finished lacing her stays and smoothing the folds of her morning gown, Catharine could no longer stand the confines of the room, where everything smelled of *him.* The sheets, the robe, the pillow she'd clung to in the dark, it was all still *his,* and it bore the unbearable memory of a night that clearly meant more to her than it ever had to him.

Her ankle throbbed dully beneath her skirts as she rose, a reminder of the fall, of the moment his arms had caught her before the world went black. The bandage tugged with every step, but she clenched her jaw and refused to limp.

She would not sit in this chamber all day, steeping in silence and weakness.

Descending the staircase was slow because each step needed to be measured and calculated to conceal the strain. She passed no one in the halls; not even the servants dared to remark on the early hour or her quiet fury. When she reached the kitchens, she startled the cook and two scullery maids, who dropped their spoons at the sight of her.

"Good morning," she told them, then she busied herself with the teacups, not really knowing what exactly she wanted to do with them. All she knew was that she needed to do *something.*

She was pouring boiling water with unsteady fingers when a voice spoke from somewhere behind her.

"Cathy."

Catharine continued to pour. "Would you like some tea?"

"You should rest." Isadora ignored the question. "That ankle—"

"Is fine," Catharine cut her off, though it was not done unkindly. "But thank you for your concern."

"I know that tone," Isadora replied, walking around the small table until she was facing Catharine. "You sometimes forget I am a woman, too, it seems. That ankle is not fine, just like *you* are not fine."

Catharine set the kettle down with more force than necessary. "It's nothing."

Isadora's voice gentled. "He'll be back."

That pronoun hung in the air like smoke.

"I didn't ask." Catharine tried to sound indifferent, but it was a futile effort.

"No. But you're playing martyr beautifully, I must say."

"I'm not waiting for him, you know. And before you dare to make that assumption, I am not heartsick." Her voice cut sharper than she meant, but she couldn't soften it. "I just need... space. Music. Yes, music. Not silence."

Isadora said nothing more. She merely nodded once with her eyes kind and knowing. Catharine fled. She didn't limp until she was alone in the hallway.

The music room sat at the far end of the house, still shrouded in soft morning gloom. No fire had yet been lit, and the air was cool. Still, she welcomed it. Pain cleared her thoughts better than any tonic. She crossed the rug and sank down at the pianoforte, ignoring the flare of her ankle as she did. Her fingers hovered above the ivory keys, poised, but then, they fell.

The first chord was loud. It was also unforgiving.

The second one was even wilder.

That was because Catharine was not playing any piece. She couldn't have named the notes if asked to. They came in a percussive, erratic storm out of her heart, full of fury and longing and everything else she refused to say aloud.

She closed her eyes, pouring herself into it, into the crash of sound and the blur of motion that allowed her to banish Alaric Vale from her mind but not from her heart. Her hands stumbled, then soared again. Notes tumbled into one another, dissonant and defiant.

With her eyes still closed, she imagined his hand on her waist, his voice in the dark. And she was overwhelmed by the empty space he had left behind. She opened her eyes immediately as her foot stepped on the pedal. Her ankle screamed in protest, but she couldn't stop.

Let the house hear. Let them all hear, she thought to herself.

She wasn't a statue. She wasn't a prize. She was a person, angry and hurt, and impossibly, dangerously alive, all because of him.

She had no idea how long she had been playing. For all she knew, it could have been an entire lifetime. The final chord rang out and echoed against the walls, trembling just like her hands. That was when she noticed him.

He had been standing in the threshold, shadowed by the dim corridor behind him. He was the dark silhouette in a now quiet room, which still echoed with the remnants of her fury. He was back.

Her spine straightened in instinctive defence. Her mask snapped into place like armour polished to a cruel shine. He took one step in, his silver-grey eyes sweeping the room, then landing on her.

"I'd say I caught the tail end of a sonata," he said with a self-satisfied smirk, "but it sounded more like a declaration of war."

She moved towards the door, ignoring the pulse leaping at the base of her throat. He stepped aside just enough to let her pass, but his presence filled the space too closely. She brushed against him, barely, but it still burned.

"You shouldn't listen at doors," she told him with a pout.

"And for a woman who doesn't care," he murmured, tilting his head, "you play remarkably bitter notes."

That statement made her stop. She turned around, aiming her eyes at him, like frost-laced glass.

"You think too highly of yourself, Lord Ravensedge." Her voice sliced like a whip. "If I played bitter notes, that was only because I enjoy dissonance, and *not* because I was grieving your absence in any way."

His lips curved into a faintest smile. "Of course. How silly of me to think otherwise." He took a step closer to her as he spoke. "You play the pianoforte like a general marshal troops. Very... detached."

Her nostrils flared. "You mistake strength for detachment."

"No," he said softly, stepping even closer. "I know exactly what it is. I just wonder if you know the difference anymore."

The air between them snapped taut. Heat pulsed in the quiet. She could hear her own heartbeat.

"You think you know me," she breathed, the words meant to wound. "But you don't."

"No," he said. "But by God, how much I want to..."

That stopped her in her tracks. She hated herself that he had such an effect on her, but as silence bloomed between them, she knew that she should have walked away, but instead, she reached for him. Or perhaps, he reached first... not that it mattered.

What mattered was the collision of their lips with the full weight of everything unspoken. It was a collision of pain and defiance and wanting, all condensed into a single, breathless moment that stretched into infinity. His hand tangled in her hair while her fingers gripped the lapel of his coat, bringing him even closer.

His hands clamped her waist, lifting her up, and without thinking, her legs encircled him. Without breaking the kiss, he pressed her against the piano, and an explosion of notes filled the space around them. But neither of them paid any attention to that.

Her fingers caressed his chin, his neck, feeling the hardness of his manhood press against the folds of her gown. Heat unfurled from somewhere deep inside of her, and suddenly, she felt both brazen and ravenous for him, for his touch, for his kisses.

He lifted the folds of her gown between them as his fingers gently trailed an invisible line down the insides of her thighs. When she felt his touch on her most intimate place, warmth overwhelmed her.

"Oh..." she moaned loudly, biting her lower lip.

His hand upon her was nothing she could ever have imagined. Her body was trembling, her thighs pulsating. The tip of his finger prodded her gently. He pulled away from her, his lips wet and his eyes on fire. He was watching her, grinning.

Her trembling fingers caressed his cheek. His fingers made tantalizing circles, a featherlight caress that made her body explode into a million sensations all at once. Strangely, she wanted to feel his fingers inside of her, and not only that. The thought made her blush underneath his steady gaze.

He leaned in to kiss her again as his words broke through the kiss.

"Should I stop?" he teased.

"No..." she managed to muster through the onslaught of pleasure. "Please..."

"Good," he murmured into her neck, inhaling her scent.

He was playing her like a virtuoso plays a finely tuned instrument. His every movement, his every kiss brought forth more sensations, creating avalanches of delight, burying her deep underneath. He started to move his fingers faster, sliding into her, and it made her tremble even more than before.

"I love how wet you are..." she heard him whisper right into her ear, and suddenly, something snapped inside of her.

Bliss overwhelmed her while her heart pounded, and all she could see before her eyes was the explosion of a million little stars. While she was still shaking from ecstasy, she felt the tip of his manhood pressing against her throbbing bud.

"Tell me if I am hurting you," he murmured tenderly.

She grabbed him by the cheeks, only to pull him close to herself. "You could never hurt me..."

A newfound tidal wave of tenderness for her husband completely seized her. She spread her legs even more as her hands clung to him. All she could feel, all she could think about, was *him,* what he was doing to her.

He slid only a little inside. Pleasure unfurled. Then he went in deeper. A little more, and he was all the way inside of her, making them one.

"Are you all right?" he asked breathlessly.

"Wonderful." She kissed him through her words. "Take me, Alaric..."

That was all she needed to tell him. He groaned through their kiss, then started to move, claiming all of her for his own. She clutched at him without thinking, pushing herself into him, giving all of herself to him. It seemed to last forever, this pleasure, when he stilled and tightened his body, only to relax a moment later, still breathing heavily.

He kissed her on the forehead, then gently moved away from her, adjusting his trousers. When their eyes locked again, they were both smiling.

"Admit it, you *were* waiting for me," he teased her playfully.

"Maybe," she replied mischievously. "But... where were you all morning?"

He shrugged. "A lord's business is never-ending, you know this." He kissed her again on the lips, just a peck, then inhaled deeply. "I will be in my study, darling."

Upon those words, he closed the door behind him. And although her heart and body were full, her mind was still racing with concern.

Chapter Twenty-Three

"He's too careful," Ashbourne stated. "That's the problem. He never writes his own orders."

The air in the study had thickened, scented with tobacco smoke, scorched wax, and the weight of consequence. The heavy curtains shut out the morning sun, but for all the men cared, it could have been midnight.

Alaric was standing near the table where the map was strewn open with his hands braced on its edge and his silvery eyes fixated on the letter that Ashbourne had dropped between them a moment ago. It was a single sheet of cream paper with four names on it. It was just a glimpse of the rot beneath Blackmoor's charm.

Still, it was not enough.

Ashbourne, poised as ever in his charcoal coat, claimed the wing-backed chair like a throne with his long legs crossed. Dorian was the one pacing about. He could never sit down during meetings like this. He was always moving, always coiled with energy barely held in check. His tawny hair was slightly dishcvcled, and his cravat loosened just enough to suggest he'd lost patience with appearances.

"Then we force his hand," Dorian said. "Get him to name something, to put something in writing, and lure him into confidence."

Alaric didn't look up. "He doesn't trust anyone enough for that. And even if he did, it wouldn't be him holding the quill."

Ashbourne nodded, folding his still gloved hands. "Precisely. That's why we use what we have. The stablehand, the payment trail, the threats. We let the whispers spread, discreetly. We suggest, not accuse. And we wait for him to start panicking."

"He won't panic," Alaric said, finally lifting his head. "He'll lash out."

Dorian paused mid-step. "Good. Let him."

Alaric's gaze drifted to the fire. He could still feel Catharine's lips on his. He could still feel the taste of truth between them. It had changed something in him, but not in a way that softened him—rather in a way that her love anchored him. Blackmoor had nearly taken her away from him. He had targeted her, albeit by mistake, and for that, Alaric was adamant to make him pay.

"We have to bring the stablehand before the magistrate," Alaric urged. "And have his statement sealed by someone not in Blackmoor's pocket."

Ashbourne raised a brow. "And who would that be? Half the circuit justices owe him favours or funding."

"I know one," Alaric said after a moment's thought. "Lord Chalcombe. He was my father's man. He hates politics, but he hates Blackmoor more."

Ashbourne considered it, then he gave a nod of agreement.

"And after?" Dorian asked. "When Blackmoor catches wind?"

"Then we let him come," Alaric replied. "Let him bribe or threaten or hire his way through every street in London. He *will* slip."

There was a short silence.

Then Rhys stood, brushing invisible dust from his sleeve. "This will get ugly."

"It already is," Alaric murmured.

A knock on the door interrupted them.

"Yes?" Alaric called out, only to find Catharine standing in the doorway in deep blue, a shade that caught the morning light and turned it storm-dark. Her hair was half-coiled, an elegant arrangement that could not disguise the slight paleness of her cheeks or the limp she still carried, however dignified.

He opened his mouth to say something, he just wasn't certain what—but she had already stepped forward. Her gaze swept the study in a glance. No one moved. She didn't speak, nor did she ask for permission.

She took in the scene with the precision of a woman trained from birth to dissect social rooms and battlefields in equal measure. Her eyes moved to the table, to the papers Alaric and the others had been parsing for hours, which consisted of bank records, sealed correspondence, estate permits bearing mismatched handwriting and forged seals. Ashbourne had been thorough in his inquiries.

Then she came to the name. Her brows knitted just slightly, but she betrayed no more than that. She stepped closer, cloaked in the silence which was thick around her, broken only by the faint crinkle of parchment beneath her fingers as she reached out and turned a letter towards her for better reading.

Ashbourne said nothing, but Alaric saw the glance he exchanged with Dorian. It was brief and pointed, a silent exchange of conclusions because she wasn't just noticing the evidence. She was *understanding* it, completely and utterly.

Catharine surveyed the forged estate transfer. Her eyes narrowed just slightly at the shifting signature. Then she took in the second document, which was a coded letter with mild language but still laced with veiled threats and impossible recommendations. Her jaw set.

She picked up a page halfway through the stack, one listing an irregular payment through a shipping firm out of Bristol.

"How many aliases has he used?" she asked quietly.

Alaric blinked.

"He... two confirmed. Possibly three," he said, slower than usual.

She nodded once, already moving on. "He's filtering through intermediaries, shell firms, and stewards. It's sloppier than I expected. Arrogant men rarely cover their tracks well."

Ashbourne tilted his head. "You read faster than I do."

She didn't look at him. "I taught myself more than to merely walk in straight lines and wear French silk, you know."

Dorian let out a breath that might have been a laugh if the tension weren't so thick. Alaric moved towards her. The instinct was immediate and primal; he needed her *out* of this and away from the paper trail that led to violence.

He was half a step away from her when she looked up and stopped him dead. Her look was steady and proud. It was daring him to underestimate her. It froze him in place.

He could have asked her to leave. She would have walked out with her head still held high, probably without a single word said. But she wouldn't have forgiven him for it... ever. That was the moment he truly understood that she wasn't a porcelain doll, that she wasn't someone to be protected in silence. She was standing here with her ankle still slightly swollen and pain etched around her eyes, and she was *choosing* this.

"Catharine..." he began quietly.

She spoke before he could finish. "If you're going to make war on a peer of the realm, Alaric, do it properly. And not alone."

Ashbourne made a small, approving noise and leaned back into his chair. Dorian smirked outright. Alaric watched her, and he knew that she wasn't asking for his permission. So despite everything in him that longed to shield her from this, he knew one thing with clarity: She could do this... she *would* do this. And he gave a nod.

Dorian handed her the folded note without hesitation. That alone told Alaric how quickly the tide was turning in this room. There had been no teasing preamble, no sly remark, just a simple, silent offering of trust.

She opened the note with her usual precision, surveying the names with narrowed eyes. Alaric watched her expression sharpen not with surprise but with calculation. Each name transformed into a subtle association, which was already spinning itself into something cohesive behind her pale eyes.

"She's frighteningly good at this," Dorian muttered beneath his breath, mostly to Alaric. "You might've married a strategist."

Alaric gave him a withering glance but said nothing. His gaze was still on her.

Rhys, standing now near the cabinet with a glass in hand, added a second paper to the table with two fingers. "And this one. Lord Tavington. He owes five thousand to one of Blackmoor's merchant fronts. That debt's been keeping his votes compliant for the last year."

Catharine moved to the firelight with both sheets of paper in hand. Her lips parted slightly as she read, her thumb pressing lightly into the corner of the page.

"Expose him in the House of Lords."

The room stilled. Ashbourne turned his head towards her with a look of confusion on his face. Even Dorian stopped mid-sip. Alaric's stomach coiled, made of equal parts dread and admiration.

"It's bold," she went on. "But not reckless. If we present the evidence formally, on the floor, during the next vote, Blackmoor can't bury it, not if it's spoken into the record in full view of the chamber. And if we time it right, we'll have enough sympathetic peers to demand an investigation."

Ashbourne tilted his head slightly. "It will be a scandal."

"It needs to be," she replied.

Dorian gave a low whistle. "You want to drag him into sunlight."

"I want to leave him nowhere to run."

Alaric studied her, not just the words she'd said but the steadiness behind them. Her voice did not shake. Her gaze did not flinch. She stood in a room full of powerful men, all trained in war and politics, and she had laid down a sharper strategy than any of them had yet spoken aloud.

She was remarkable. And she was right.

"It's dangerous," Alaric said quietly. "You know that."

She turned her gaze to him then, something steady and unspoken passing between them.

"So is doing nothing."

He stepped closer to her, but he didn't say anything.

Ashbourne nodded once, final and clean. "Then it's settled. If we do this, it must be ironclad. And we'll have to go now if we're to make the chamber before the roll is called."

Dorian straightened his cuffs, already halfway to the door. "I still say it's not truly a lords' session if half of them are still sleeping off last night's brandy."

Ashbourne merely gave him a look and crossed to collect the sealed documents they had prepared in advance.

Alaric turned towards Catharine, foolishly expecting that she might return to the drawing room or perhaps remain behind with Isadora, out of the line of fire. Instead, she had already donned her gloves.

"I'm coming," she said simply.

He paused. "Catharine—"

Her chin lifted in defiance. "You've brought me into this. I've seen the papers. I helped plan the strategy. I'm not going to sit by the window and wait to hear what becomes of it."

Alaric exhaled slowly. There was no heat in her tone, only clarity, making it not a plea but a firm decision.

"You do know women aren't permitted in the chamber," he reminded her.

"I know," she replied. "So does every man who will whisper about it."

Ashbourne turned from the cabinet with the barest flicker of interest behind his pale eyes.

Dorian grinned. "This'll be fun."

Alaric watched Catharine's pale eyes, which dared him to argue. He didn't.

"Very well," he said. "You'll ride with me."

She nodded once, and it felt like a declaration between generals. They made for the carriage in a tight procession. Alaric helped her in first, noting how she leaned less on her injured ankle today, though the tension in her jaw betrayed the pain. She didn't speak of it, and he didn't mention it.

"You're aware this will cause talk," he said softly.

She turned her head towards him. "Good."

He gave a low laugh. "You want to make a statement."

"So do you," she said evenly. "You're taking me with you."

He looked at her then as if he were seeing her for the first time, and she was utterly breathtaking.

"Yes," he said. "I am."

And that was the end of it.

As the carriage pulled into the courtyard of Westminster, the liveried footmen outside the House of Lords slowed their movements, utterly confused by the sight. Their eyes slid towards the door as Alaric stepped out, then extended his hand towards the woman inside.

Gasps did not carry far in a London morning, but glances did.

When Catharine Fairbourne Vale, Marchioness of Ravensedge, descended the carriage steps beside her husband and walked with him towards the entrance of the lords' chamber, every man watching understood one thing clearly.

This was not a mistake. This was a *message.*

And somewhere in the heart of that ancient building, Lord Blackmoor was about to learn that his war had become a reckoning.

Chapter Twenty-Four

The air inside the House of Lords was not meant for women. Catharine felt it the moment she crossed the threshold.

It was colder here, not in temperature but in tone, for it was a space carved of ancient stone and older rules, and the very architecture seemed to protest her presence, as if the heavy columns and echoing ceilings bristled at the sight of skirts sweeping over sacred ground.

And yet she walked.

Dozens of gazes turned towards her at once. Some were merely curious, while others were utterly disapproving. A few were brimming with barely veiled disdain, and they didn't bother to lower their voices.

"Is that Lady Ravensedge?"

"A woman in the lords' vestibule... impossible!"

"Shameless, truly. She must be hysterical or worse—ambitious."

She heard every word, and she let them slide across her skin like dull blades. Her spine stayed straight, and her chin lifted higher.

And Alaric did not flinch. His gait was steady beside hers, as if he were escorting a duchess into a ballroom and not defying centuries of protocol. He offered no apology, no glance to the crowd. His hand rested lightly on her back, and it was not possessive but grounding, as if to say: *This is my wife, and she belongs exactly here, by my side, for where I go, she goes, too.*

And perhaps, Catharine thought, she did.

They passed through the vestibule, towards the narrower corridor where peers gathered before entering the chamber itself. Rich voices rumbled low in conversation, some already tinged with the tension of what was coming.

Ashbourne waited by the far doors, flanked by Dorian, and both men were seen speaking to a clerk who did not look pleased. When Ashbourne spotted her, he gave a faint nod, but in his eyes, she caught the edge of approval.

She didn't need it, but it was still welcome, for the weight of her presence there was deliberate and calculated. And yet as she stood among titled men in their tailored coats and polished shoes, surrounded by old marble and even older eyes, a cold knot twisted in her chest.

She had walked into drawing rooms filled with dukes and diplomats. She had hosted charity galas beside viscountesses and foreign princes. She had known every form of society's scrutiny. But this was different.

This was patriarchal power, and she was trespassing.

Alaric leaned close, his voice just above a whisper. "We can still say the word and leave."

Catharine didn't look at him.

"No," she refuted. "Let them see. Let them *remember*."

The double doors opened, and the hall beyond was a deep well of red and gold and judgment. She could not follow him into the chamber itself, but she would remain here, in this liminal space, visible and present.

That was when a whisper reached her ear, sharp as a blade.

"Poor thing," came the voice. "They always break in the end, don't they?" Laughter followed those words, mean and bitter.

Then she heard her name. "Lady Ravensedge."

It was drawn out in a mocking hush, laced with the sickly sweetness of courtesy. She turned, and there he was.

Lord Blackmoor.

He lounged near a column like a man entirely at ease, the velvet of his coat catching the candlelight. But it was his eyes, and the gleaming in them, smug, feral, and far too pleased with himself.

He didn't bow, and he didn't blink. His gaze crawled over her like oil, lingering just long enough to insult without word or gesture. The corner of his mouth twitched upward, resembling a wolf in polished boots.

"I thought you'd be tucked away," he said in a low and poisonous tone of voice. "Knitting or weeping or whatever it is fallen women do these days."

Catharine's pulse thudded in her ears. But she didn't flinch.

"You should have learned by now, my lord," she replied coolly, "that women don't break. Not the ones that the likes of you fear."

His smile faltered, just barely, but Alaric was there by her side, a man carved from granite itself. The hall fell quieter by degrees.

Catharine's eyes did not leave Blackmoor's face, but Blackmoor wasn't watching her anymore. He was listening, and he did not like what he heard.

"My lords," Alaric began, "I come not with accusations born of rumour, but with evidence, signed, sealed, and witnessed."

He held up a folded page. His thumb tapped its edge once.

"This," he said, "is the testimony of Mr. Thomas Richards, formerly employed as a stablehand at the Fairbourne estate. Three nights ago, he confessed, under oath and without coercion, that he was paid to sabotage a lady's saddle. The coin passed through three hands, but he traced it back to Lord Blackmoor's agent."

A stir rippled across the chamber. He passed the testimony to the clerk. No one looked away. Alaric didn't pause.

"This morning, a magistrate of no political allegiance signed this account. It has been sealed and witnessed."

Ashbourne stepped forward, laying the next document on the long table.

"The estate documents," Ashbourne said crisply. "Filed three months ago, approved with a forged permit bearing the crest of Lord Blackmoor's household. The steward who signed it fled to Bath last month, but we have his confession. This is his handwriting. But not his words."

Another parchment followed.

"The financial trail is... inelegant," he continued. "Bank drafts drawn through shell firms and payments masked as agricultural expansion, which were conveniently routed through shipping companies Blackmoor's cousin directs."

A murmur rose. Alaric let it swell. Then silenced it with his next words.

"This letter," he said, lifting another sheet, "was found among the papers of Lord Halberton, a minor peer who abstained from a trade vote last season. Weeks later, his debts were called in. He received this shortly before."

He held it aloft, then read. "It would be unfortunate if your holdings at Caversham were to fall into disrepair... accidents are so common among poorly managed estates."

Alaric lowered the page.

"The letter is unsigned. But the seal on the envelope matches that of Lord Blackmoor's private office. The clerk of this house has verified it."

The clerk stood, a pale man with careful eyes. "Confirmed. The seal is authentic."

Blackmoor surged forward.

"This is a farce!" he snapped. "A campaign of slander from a disgraced officer and his radical allies. You bring the word of a *servant* into this chamber?"

Alaric turned to face him with a voice like thunder. "We bring *truth*, Blackmoor. And unlike you, we do not pay for silence."

Another lord leaned forward. "Is the steward's confession available?"

Ashbourne bowed slightly. "It will be submitted by noon."

And then, there was a charged, crackling hush. Pages passed hand to hand. Whispers rose, hushed and urgent.

Blackmoor stepped forward. His voice, when he finally spoke, was smoother than Catharine expected. It was practiced and coated in something that might have passed for dignity to those who hadn't just watched him unravel.

"My lords," he began, spreading his hands in a gesture too theatrical to be genuine, "surely you must see what this is: political manoeuvring. A coordinated attack from men who have much to gain if I fall."

A few of the older lords shifted, looking uncomfortable.

"I have served in commerce, in diplomacy," Blackmoor continued. "Yes, my dealings have been complex, but none of them were illegal. I've made enemies, certainly. That is the price of ambition. But forgery?" He gave a practiced scoff. "Bribery? Sabotage? Do you truly believe I'd stoop so low?"

Catharine watched his eyes. They darted everywhere, calculating a way out. He was desperate to measure the weight of the room, to find some corner still under his influence.

"I don't deny acquaintance with the men mentioned," he went on. "But the documents are circumstantial and misinterpreted. I had no knowledge of any servant's actions—"

Ashbourne's voice cut in, cool as steel. "Your steward signed the property transfer. You threatened Lord Halberton with foreclosure. Shall we read your cousin's letter aloud?"

Blackmoor ignored him. He raised his voice, fuller now and louder, as if he believed sheer force could drown the evidence.

"This is the cost of refusing to bend to the whims of petty peers, of speaking truth in the chamber. I have always acted in service to the Crown—"

"Enough," Alaric said, quiet and lethal.

It wasn't a shout. It didn't need to be.

Blackmoor turned to him. "You have no authority to condemn me."

"No," Alaric replied. "But the truth does."

Blackmoor's face tightened. Catharine noticed a twitch at the corner of his mouth, then a bead of sweat at his temple.

His posture stiffened, as if his carefully cultivated composure were a mask unravelling at the edges.

She knew that look. She had seen it once before, years ago, in a man who'd lost a hand of cards and decided the rules no longer applied. The predator's mask had slipped.

And then chaos ensued.

It happened too fast. She heard a sudden shout, followed by the sound of a chair being knocked back. She detected the rush of bodies moving too slowly. And Blackmoor, she realised then, wasn't going for Alaric.

He was coming for *her.*

Chapter Twenty-Five

Alaric saw it before anyone else did.

"Catharine!" Alaric shouted, then moved immediately.

It was instinct, refined over years on the battlefield, where danger often arrived on the back of silence, not noise. Alaric's spine snapped taut. Something in the air broke, and an intelligible voice shouted from somewhere behind him, but the words were lost in the sudden roar of motion.

Alaric's vision tunnelled. The entire world narrowed to the flash of Blackmoor's hand reaching forward and the shape of Catharine standing alone at the edge of the vestibule. Alaric could see her body frozen in that split second of terrible recognition.

She couldn't move fast enough to avoid Blackmoor's attack, so Alaric had to.

He launched himself across the space with the force of a man possessed. The impact was a bone-jarring crack as he tackled Blackmoor mid-lunge, with his shoulder crashing into the man's ribs with enough power to drive the air from both their lungs. They hit the floor hard, feeling the unforgiving stone beneath them.

Blackmoor twisted beneath him like a serpent.

"You bastard," the man spat wildly. "You think you've won—"

Alaric's fist silenced him. The first blow was clean, while the second broke skin. By the third, Alaric wasn't thinking anymore. He was *feeling*.

Rage surged through him like unrelenting wildfire. Every whispered slur Blackmoor had ever spoken was now inside Alaric's mind. Every time Catharine had been looked at like property, like leverage, like less surfaced as well.

His knuckles split. Blood, whether it was Blackmoor's or his own, he didn't know, spattered across polished marble.

"You came at her?" he growled between blows. "You came to her? You think that was ever going to end well for you?"

Blackmoor swung wildly, landing a glancing hit to Alaric's side. Then another to his jaw, but it barely registered. The pain was distant, swallowed by fury. Alaric pinned him again, grabbed the front of his coat, and drove him back down with a violent crack of skull against stone.

"I'll see you hang for this," Blackmoor gasped, his face slick with blood and spit.

"No," Alaric snarled with his teeth bared. "You'll live with it. That's the better punishment."

A bootstep thundered beside him.

"Alaric, that's enough!" Ashbourne was, as always, the voice of reason, and it came just in time.

Hands gripped Alaric's arm, pulling him back. Alaric resisted, feeling one last swing coiled in his muscles, but Ashbourne wrenched harder.

"You've made your point," Ashbourne insisted. "If you keep going, they'll arrest *you* next."

Alaric froze at those words. His fists still shook. His chest heaved like he'd run a cavalry charge, but Ashbourne's voice reached through the haze.

Slowly, Alaric let Blackmoor drop.

The man slumped against the marble, bloodied and gasping, one eye already swelling shut, a tooth broken and pink foam bubbling at the edge of his sneer. The guards surged in then, liveried and stern, as they seized the disgraced lord by both arms. Blackmoor didn't fight them, but he didn't stop talking. He was spitting curses, shouting threats, dragging their names through the filth, even as he was dragged from the chamber like refuse.

"You'll regret this, Vale! You think the lords will forget your whore's face in here? This little spectacle? They'll never let either of you in again—"

Alaric lunged again, but Ashbourne held him tightly. The doors slammed shut behind the guards and the writhing mess they carried between them.

That was when the world went still. Alaric hastily turned towards Catharine. She was standing exactly where she had been, though now one of her hands clutched the edge of a column. Her face was pale and her eyes wide, but not with fear. She seemed stunned into immobility, as the entire chamber watched in silence.

Alaric rushed over to her. His boots echoed over the floor as he crossed the space between them, his heart pounding harder than any fight could justify. When he reached her, he didn't touch her, although his hands reached out for her. At first, he just looked and searched her eyes, her mouth, her hands.

"You're hurt," he told her, still breathless.

"I'm not," she replied. But the tremble in her voice betrayed her.

He reached for her then, unable to help it. His hands framed her face, and his fingers trembled now that it was over.

"He... he would have..." His breath caught. "I didn't see it coming until—"

"I know," she whispered. "He looked at me like he wanted to destroy me."

Alaric's jaw clenched.

"I would've killed him."

"I know..."

She leaned into him, just slightly, but it was enough. He wrapped his arms around her, drawing her in as tightly as he could without hurting her ankle. Her hands slid to his waist, clutching the bloodied edge of his coat. He could feel her grounding herself in his heat, in his breath, and even in his fury.

"I'm not letting you out of my sight again," he murmured into her hair.

"You won't need to," she whispered back.

The doors had barely finished echoing shut when the chamber stirred again. However, this time there was the echo of something serene: recognition.

The evidence had been irrefutable. The documents, the witnesses, the numbers exposed every lie Blackmoor had wrapped himself in. Every line of ink was now a chain around his neck.

Alaric stood still, breathing hard, his hands still flexing as they came down from the violence of moments ago. Blood still cooled on his knuckles. Catharine stood beside him, her hand curled lightly around his sleeve, grounding him.

Then he noticed movement. A figure approached from the left. Lord Peregrine was old, thin, and always conservative to a fault. His expression was still strained as always, not quite ashamed but not proud either. He cleared his throat as he spoke.

"You've... served this House well today, Lord Ravensedge," he said stiffly. "It seems some of us may have been too eager to listen to rumour rather than fact."

His gaze flickered to Alaric's scar, then dropped away.

Before Alaric could respond, another stepped forward. This was Lord Greaves, a sharp-featured man who'd once openly questioned Alaric's fitness to serve. He said nothing at first, merely reached out and placed a firm hand on Alaric's shoulder. It stayed there a moment longer than expected.

"I was wrong," Greaves murmured. "And you were right to be angry."

Alaric nodded once. He wasn't sure he could speak without his voice cracking. A few more followed: Lord Melcombe, Lord Harrow, even the famously disdainful Lord Rowntree, who had once referred to him in print as *a scarred mongrel in a nobleman's coat*. Now the man offered a silent nod, but none of them looked at Catharine. Their eyes slid past her as though they didn't quite know how to confront what her presence had meant, how wrong they'd all been. But their nods towards Alaric carried more than just respect now. There was regret in it, and even more importantly, a promise.

They wouldn't turn their backs on him again.

Dorian joined them, while Ashbourne lingered behind with his arms crossed, still watching the doors, as if daring someone else to try anything stupid. Alaric looked towards the Speaker of the Lords, who had resumed his place at the dais. The man cleared his throat with a weary finality.

"Let the record reflect," he said, "that Lord Blackmoor's testimony is stricken from the proceedings, and the matter shall be turned over to the Crown's judicial authority. An inquiry will follow. If additional evidence supports collusion against the integrity of this chamber..." He paused. "Treason will be considered."

Catharine turned her head slightly towards Alaric and spoke just loud enough for him to hear.

"You've done it."

He shook his head faintly. "*We* have."

She didn't argue. They stood in the centre of the chamber like a fault line, visible and undeniable. Several minutes later, Alaric fell into step beside Catharine as they exited the House of Lords. The heavy doors closed behind them with a sound that seemed to seal away the day's chaos. Behind, Ashbourne and Dorian lingered with the other lords. Alaric didn't look back.

The London air was crisp with the scent of rain from earlier in the day, and the streetlamps cast pools of golden light on the wet cobblestones. Catharine walked beside him, steady despite the lingering ache in her ankle.

At the carriage, the coachman tipped his hat in respectful silence. Alaric helped Catharine up the steps, steadying her hand on his arm. Once seated, the carriage door closed softly behind them, muffling the sounds of the city and the gathering dusk.

He sat close, their knees brushing under the lantern's glow. The carriage jolted into motion, into a steady rhythm that somehow calmed the storm in his chest.

"Thank you," he said quietly.

She smiled. "For what?"

"For not turning away," he replied, his fingers twitching as if to reach for her, but unsure if she would let him.

She didn't speak. Instead, when the carriage slowed near Ravensedge Hall, he leaned in. His hand brushed a stray lock of chestnut hair from her face, and her thumb traced the line of her jaw. The moment stretched, fraught and fragile. Then, slowly, he lowered his mouth to hers.

The kiss was soft at first, hesitant, as if both were unsure whether this was reality or some dream born from adrenaline and relief. But then it deepened into something fierce and certain, something that spoke of battles fought and won, of scars seen and shared, and finally, of a future which was still uncertain but at the same time undeniable.

When they finally parted, Alaric rested his forehead against hers.

"It's over," he whispered.

She smiled back, almost shyly. "And something else is just beginning."

Shortly after, they stood in the quiet warmth of Ravensedge Hall. The weight of the day's battles lingered in the stillness between them, binding them together in a fragile, unspoken alliance.

And for now, in the safety of these walls, that recognition was enough. It was a beginning, not of forgiveness, but of truth finally spoken aloud. And sometimes, truth was the sharpest kind of power that led to peace and love.

Chapter Twenty-Six

The grand ballroom shimmered with opulence, every crystal chandelier casting prismatic light over gilded mouldings and polished marble floors. Catharine stood at the heart of it all, draped in silver silk that caught the light like moonbeams woven into fabric.

This was her triumph.

The air hummed with whispered admiration and cautious approval. Nobles who had once glanced at them both with thinly veiled doubt now sought their attention, their smiles carefully calibrated to appear warm yet respectful. She could feel their eyes tracing her from head to toe, measuring her worth not just as a wife to the Marquess of Ravensedge but as a woman who had taken her place and now owned it.

A faint pulse of satisfaction stirred within her, but beneath it lay a tighter coil of tension. The silk felt heavier than it should have, as if the weight of all those gazes was pressing against her skin.

Her mind flickered back to the whispered scandals she had silenced, the nights she had spent crying, the shadow of shame which had finally been lifted from her family's name. All of it had led to this moment, a moment she had once thought impossible.

"Ah, there she is," a voice called, musical and amused.

Catharine turned just as Lady Leclair arrived in a flourish of dark violet skirts and dramatic sleeves, her fan snapping open like the wing of some decadent bird.

"Well, *Lady Davis*," Lady Leclair said, bowing with exaggerated formality, "how very tasteful of you to steal the entire evening."

The name landed between them like a dropped jewel, brilliant and sharp with memory.

Catharine's lips curved before she could help it. "Lady Leclair," she murmured, dipping into a curtsey so refined it might have been taught by angels.

There was something deeply comforting in this private moment they shared. Lady Leclair, for all her scandalous edge and theatrical flair, saw more than most. Then, just as swiftly as she had arrived, she was gone, swept back into the crowd like a wisp of velvet and perfume and laughter.

That was when a small group of lords and ladies swept towards her with smiles bright but guarded, making her forget all about Lady Leclair.

"Lady Ravensedge," Lady Penelope Ashford said, her voice smooth as silk, "what a splendid ball you and the marquess have thrown. The evening sparkles as much as your gown."

Lady Ashford's eyes held a glimmer of genuine admiration, though tempered by the ever-present wariness society reserved for a woman who had risen too swiftly. Catharine knew that it would probably take some more time for everyone to realise the mistake of their haughtiness. But she was willing to let bygones be bygones, as long as she had her husband by her side. Still, they were all trying, and that counted for something.

Lord Haverford, a tall and stern man with silvering hair, inclined his head. "Indeed. The arrangements were impeccable, my lady. The music, the lighting... events like this remind one of the grandeur this house deserves."

A gentleman beside him, Lord Whitby, added with a polite bow, "Your Ladyship's tact and grace have turned many sceptics into admirers. The courage to stand beside Lord Ravensedge in the House of Lords... it has not gone unnoticed."

Catharine's lips curved in a subtle but grateful smile. "Your kindness honours me, my lords and ladies. But none of this would have been possible without Lord Ravensedge."

She allowed warmth into her tone, which a reminder that, while she stood here alone for now, this victory was shared.

Lady Ashford's gaze flickered towards the gathering crowd, then back to Catharine. "There are still whispers, of course. But tonight, those whispers falter beneath the clamour of your triumph."

Catharine nodded, her thoughts a flicker behind her composed mask.

Let them whisper.

Before another word could be exchanged, the soft murmur of the orchestra swelled, and the crowd gently parted, drawing the lords and ladies away to other conversations and dances. Catharine took a steadying breath, feeling the pulse of the evening thrumming in the air.

Suddenly, a voice came from somewhere behind her.

"Triumphant, my dear. Absolutely, devastatingly triumphant!"

Catharine turned around, only to face a smiling Isadora. "You flatter me." She smiled.

"I merely state facts," Isadora replied, sweeping into place beside her, her pale blue gown catching the light in soft waves. "Half the room is still breathless from that waltz set. And the other half is pretending not to be."

Catharine allowed herself a quiet moment of pure joy. "Thank you," she said, utterly sincerely. "Truly. This evening means more than you could ever imagine."

Isadora nudged her lightly with her elbow. "Because it's your and Alaric's victory. And no one would dare pretend otherwise."

They stood shoulder to shoulder, two women who had withstood far more than anyone here would ever know, surveying the ballroom like generals after battle. Then a flicker of movement across the room caught Isadora's attention. Her gaze sharpened, even locked. Catharine followed it and nearly smiled.

There, near the tall windows, stood Alaric and Dorian Gainsworth. Her husband's dark, broad frame cut a striking silhouette even in the shadows. He stood in half-profile, nodding at something Dorian was saying with his arms crossed and his posture completely relaxed but alert. Dorian, ever dashing, was gesturing animatedly, all devil-may-care charm and golden wit.

Isadora's eyes did not leave them.

Catharine tilted her head, her smile a wicked gleam of mischief. "You're staring."

"I am *not*," Isadora sniffed, though her gaze hadn't budged. "I was simply observing the uhm... fine tailoring of Lord Gainsworth's coat."

Catharine nearly choked on her champagne. "Oh, so it's the *coat* that has your attention? Not the man in it?"

Isadora rolled her eyes, her cheeks flushing the faintest shade of pink. "He's arrogant."

"He's handsome," Catharine countered.

"He's incorrigible."

"He keeps you on your toes."

That earned her a long look. Then, in a voice only slightly begrudging, Isadora murmured a confession. "I might possibly… *possibly*… be fond of Dorian Gainsworth."

Catharine lifted a hand to her chest in mock surprise. "Heavens. It would seem I need smelling salts from the shock of this news."

Isadora's lips twitched. "Do not make me regret confiding in you."

They both laughed then, huddled together.

"But in all fairness," Catharine added, sipping from her glass, "fondness looks suspiciously like open warfare, in your case."

"Oh, absolutely," Isadora agreed, sweeping a curl behind her ear. "We're perfectly dreadful to each other. It's practically courtship."

Catharine grinned. "Then I wish you both a very long and bloody one."

"I shall treasure that blessing always."

They clinked glasses in a quiet toast to the strange shape love sometimes took: stubborn, sharp-edged, and fiercely earned.

Unexpectedly, the violins shifted just for a breath, and then they stopped altogether. The sound ceased suddenly, all at once, leaving only the hush of silence and expectant gazes.

Catharine and Isadora turned their heads instinctively. Alaric stood there, across the chamber, just beyond the marble arch at the end of the ballroom. The crowd subtly parted around him as if space itself had bent to make way for him. He didn't move at first. He only looked at her, finding her among a million other faces, wanting and needing only her.

Then he spoke in a manner that was not loud or theatrical. His voice didn't ring like a rehearsed toast or a speech meant to charm. It was something far rarer among such a crowd. It was something *honest,* something deep and filled with a truth that settled into the very marrow of each word spoken.

"I love you," he said simply, looking at no one and nothing but her.

The words were not embellished; there was no poetry in them. Yet they were the most beautiful words she had ever heard.

"I have fought wars," Alaric continued, his voice low but heard in every corner of the grand ballroom. "I have ridden into chaos with no certainty of return. But nothing... *nothing* has ever terrified me more than loving you. And nothing has ever mattered more."

A soft gasp rippled through the crowd, but no one interrupted. A few of the ladies pressed their hands to their chests, overwhelmed by the tenderness of the moment. Catharine herself could not move.

She felt an onslaught of tears come on, but she managed to keep them under control as Alaric continued to speak.

"I love you," Alaric said again, slower this time, as if it needed no explanation. "Not for what you've done or what you've endured, not for how the world sees you. I love you because you are *you,* because you are brave, because you are brilliant... because you are *mine.*"

The silence that followed was complete. Even the air felt reverent. The lords and ladies who had watched her with mild curiosity only minutes ago now stood like portraits, still and awestruck. There were no polite coughs, no whispered barbs.

Catharine's throat tightened, breath caught somewhere between disbelief and joy. No one had ever spoken of love like it was armour and fire all at once. No one had ever spoken it where the world could hear. But Alaric had, and it was all for her.

Guided by pure instinct, Catharine stepped forward. She didn't hesitate. She didn't think. She moved with her silver gown trailing behind her like liquid moonlight. Her path parted the onlookers like a tide. Her blood hummed in her ears. Her breath trembled, but her steps did not falter.

Alaric stood rooted, his storm-coloured eyes never leaving her face, not when she drew near, not when she stopped just before him, not even when she rose onto her toes and kissed him in front of everyone.

There was a sharp, collective breath from the crowd. They did not sound scandalised but rather stunned. Still, Catharine didn't care.

Let them watch. Let them whisper.

This moment was theirs.

"I love you, too," she whispered back as their foreheads touched.

His hands came to her waist, grounding her even as the world tilted. Her fingers found his jaw, her palm brushing the edge of his scar.

He bent his head slightly. "May I have this dance, Lady Ravensedge?"

Her lips curved. "I thought you'd never ask."

Musicians, as everyone knows, are clever creatures. They needed no cue. The violins lifted again, this time with the soft sweep of a waltz just beginning.

Alaric took her hand. His palm was warm against hers as he led her onto the dance area. They moved together in the centre of the ballroom, just the two of them. Around them, the world blurred. Her skirts spun in silver arcs while his hold on her was steady and sure.

. For a woman who had been jilted twice, who had once thought love a dangerous, foolish thing, this felt nothing like foolishness. This felt like home.

As they danced together, the music wove around them under the gleaming chandeliers. She glanced up at him, breathless.

"Was that declaration necessary? You could have professed your love for me privately, you know," she teased. "You've turned half the duchesses faint and the other half insufferably romantic."

Alaric's mouth tilted in a half-smile. "Necessary? No. Satisfying? Absolutely."

Her lips twitched. "And what of my reputation? You've scandalised every matron on the committee for decorum."

"They'll survive," he murmured, twirling her smoothly beneath his arm. "Or retire early. I wouldn't mind either outcome."

She laughed. "Admit it, you enjoyed that far too much."

"I enjoy *you* far too much," he corrected, drawing her just a little closer with a firm hand at her waist. "You should know that by now."

Catharine tilted her head, pretending to consider. "Well, you're fortunate I'm so irresistibly charming. Imagine if I were cold and unfeeling."

"You were," he said, utterly deadpan.

She gave a mock gasp, swatting his arm lightly with her gloved hand.

"And yet," Alaric continued, leaning in, voice low near her ear, "I fell in love with you anyway. Terrifying, isn't it?"

Her heart stumbled.

"Terrifying," she agreed, barely more than a breath.

His gaze made her tremble.

"Promise me," she said suddenly. "When the music ends... you'll still be here."

He tightened his hand over hers. "I'm not going anywhere."

The music swelled towards its final measure, and they moved in perfect time, no longer two people bracing against the world but a pair finally moving with it... together.

Chapter Twenty-Seven

The rain drummed steadily against the tall windows of the study, a slow and calmly relentless rhythm that suited Alaric's mood. Outside, Ravensedge was cloaked in mist. The gardens were veiled in grey like a painting left to fade. But inside, the fire burned low and warm, casting an amber glow across the heavy oak desk littered with correspondence and opened reports. Stillness settled over the room, broken only by the quiet scratch of Alaric's pen and the occasional shift of leather as he leaned back in thought.

Suddenly, a knock interrupted his quiet moment.

"Yes?" he called out, looking up.

The butler entered with his usual precision. "My lord, there is a visitor here for you. Lord Jonathan Everley, emissary from the Privy Council. He asks for a moment of your time."

Alaric's brow rose, but he merely nodded. "Send him in."

Moments later, the door opened again to admit a man dressed in the exact sort of restraint Alaric had come to expect from men who trafficked in influence rather than conviction. He was wrapped in a dark coat with an understated cravat around his neck, every detail carefully unremarkable. Lord Everley carried himself like a blade sheathed in propriety: sharp but polished.

"Lord Ravensedge," Everley said, bowing just enough to satisfy etiquette. "Thank you for receiving me."

Alaric gestured to the seat opposite his desk. "Let's dispense with the niceties, shall we?"

Everley inclined his head, unbothered. "As you wish."

There was no preamble and no manoeuvring. The offer was laid out cleanly, like a ledger balanced in full.

"You are to be offered a seat at the Privy Council," the man stated simply.

Alaric knew what that meant: prestige, influence, and proximity to power, if not power itself. The stain of war he had been wearing like a scarlet letter would be washed clean by the hand of politics, and the rumours of his disgrace would be replaced by deference. Doors that had been bolted would open. Voices that had once whispered behind fans would greet him with bows.

But there was a catch. Of course, there was always a catch.

Everley folded his hands and looked at him directly. "Your wife's presence at the Lords and her increasingly visible role in your affairs have not gone unnoticed. It is the view of the Council that these recent public demonstrations, while not illegal, are *unconventional*. We believe your elevation would be better received if she were... softened."

Alaric said nothing, but the silence was taut.

Everley pressed on. "She need not be hidden, of course. A wife with opinions is not the scandal it once was. But society prefers its influence wielded quietly, behind fans and through husbands, not from the floor of Parliament or in published letters. A seat such as this"—he paused delicately—"requires a certain preservation of tradition."

Alaric understood exactly what the man was saying. He felt it in his bones, the press of centuries of men before him, of carved expectation and ritual. The room itself seemed to lean in, heavy with oil paintings and leather-bound legacies. For a moment, he imagined what he might gain. But at the same time, he imagined what he would lose.

Catharine's eyes, sharp as glass and twice as unyielding, immediately rose inside his mind. Then he remembered her voice, her fire, the steel beneath her grace. She had stood beside him when no one else had. She had never once asked him to shrink. And he would be damned if he ever asked it of her.

"I see," he said coolly, rising to his full height.

Everley stood as well, sensing the shift.

Everley's lips tightened. "We would expect your answer before the quarter's end."

He turned with precision and headed for the door. As soon as he reached for the handle and opened it, Alaric's voice stopped him.

"No need," Alaric said calmly. "I can give you my answer right now. No."

Everly paused mid-step and turned back. "I beg your pardon?"

Alaric straightened, his voice ironclad. "I said no. I will not accept a seat bought by the erasure of my wife's voice. I would never ask her to dim herself for the comfort of men too frightened to confront a woman with conviction."

The silence that followed was heavy, almost brittle.

Everley's expression didn't falter at all. His lips parted, but for a rare moment, he seemed at a loss.

"This is... highly unorthodox," he managed, his tone carefully even. "You do understand what you're refusing, Lord Ravensedge. Most men would not hesitate."

Alaric let out a slow breath, steady and clear. "Then most men are fools."

He moved around the desk with quiet, deliberate steps, stopping just before the window. Rain streaked down the panes like ink. Beyond them, the estate grounds stretched in soft greys and greens, blurred and beautiful.

"My life with Catharine has been unorthodox from the beginning," he said without turning. "Unorthodox when she challenged Blackmoor in public, when she stood beside me in the Lords, when she kissed me in front of half the *ton* without blinking."

He turned then, his silver-grey eyes like steel under water. "And I wouldn't change a single moment of it. I don't want a wife who knows her place... I want a partner. And if that disqualifies me from a place among your council, so be it."

Everley was still staring at him. Then, after what seemed like a small eternity of silence, he adjusted the cuffs of his gloves, and his mask slipped neatly back into place.

"I see," he said coolly. "Well. Your answer is clear."

"It is," Alaric replied.

Everley gave a short bow. "Then I shall trouble you no further."

He crossed the threshold and disappeared down the corridor. The door clicked softly shut behind him. Alaric exhaled, shoulders relaxing as though a weight had been cast off. However, it was not the weight of lost opportunity but rather of avoided compromise.

Let the Privy Council call it reckless. Let society raise its brows and sharpen its fans.

Because his wife would never be silenced, and the life they were building was worth more than every seat in every room full of men who mistook power for principle.

The study had only just fallen quiet again when the door suddenly burst open. Alaric turned instinctively, just in time to catch Catharine as she flew into the room like a gust of storm-wind and firelight. Her skirts swept behind her in a silver arc, and then she was in his arms, light and unhesitating as she threw herself against his chest and kissed him full on the mouth.

His hands closed around her waist out of instinct, grounding her as the world tilted, while he felt her lips urgent and soft and impossibly warm. She kissed him like she'd been holding something back for days, and now that restraint had shattered. Her fingers curled in his coat, and her breath tangled with his.

When she finally pulled back, he couldn't resist laughing.

"What on earth was that for?" he asked with one hand still curved protectively around the back of her neck.

Catharine was grinning, breathless and radiant, with her cheeks flushed from more than just the rush upstairs.

"I overheard," she said simply, still close enough that her words ghosted across his skin. "I was coming down the hall, and I heard everything you told that man."

Alaric blinked in surprise and then let his head fall back with a groan. "Of course you did."

"No one..." Her voice wavered, but only for a second. "No one has ever said anything like that about me... *for* me... not ever."

There was a look in her eyes he recognised all too well: disbelief, trembling at the edge of joy. That careful, tempered part of her was trying to catch up to the reality in front of her. And so he gave her something to anchor to.

"Well," he said, smiling like the devil, "I've got a few more beautiful things in mind I'd like to do to you."

Her eyes widened. She flushed deep crimson and let out a scandalised laugh. "Alaric!"

"What?" he asked innocently. "You walked in here kissing me senseless. I assumed we were making declarations."

"And what exactly are you declaring?" she asked, still breathless and still half-laughing.

Instead of answering, he pulled her tighter against him and kissed her again. This one wasn't light or teasing. It wasn't hurried or startled. This was a promise written in heat and certainty in the curl of his hand at her hip and the slow drag of his lips over hers. She melted into him, soft and eager, her arms winding around his neck.

"Let me show you." He grinned, leading her to the chaise lounge in the corner, by the bookcase, where he sat her down. Then he knelt before her.

"Alaric, what on earth…" she started, but he cut her off with just his glance.

"Shhh," he murmured, lifting up the hem of her gown, revealing the porcelain whiteness of her thighs. His manhood roared for her like a wild animal, wanting to devour her.

"No, you cannot possibly do what I think you—" Again, she was interrupted by his lips between her thighs.

"Oh…" she murmured, and the sound of her moaning made him feel instantly overwhelmed.

He showed her his tongue, which slid inside her velvet heat. She gasped, gripping a handful of his hair as if she were afraid that he might change his mind and stop kissing her. Instead, she spread her legs wider, offering herself up to him. The sight drove him mad with desire.

He sucked her into his mouth, playing with his tongue. He was pleasuring her, and yet he knew that she wanted more and more. Her entire body trembled beneath his knowing touch as his tongue kept flicking over her sensitive bud, playing with her, tormenting her.

He slid a finger inside of her, wet and hot. He, too, wanted more of her. He wanted all she had to give him. She bit her lower lip, obviously unable to control the desire he pulled out of her.

He knew exactly what he was doing, what she liked. He followed the rhythm of her body like music. And it didn't take him long to make her insides clench, then explode into a wetness that leaped out of her very core. But he didn't stop licking her, sucking her, keeping the heat steady and ongoing. His tongue was buried deep inside of her, lapping up the delectable wetness of her very being.

Then she grabbed him by the cheeks and made him look up.

"I want you," she murmured, blushing, but the desire to show him was stronger and overpowering.

He grinned. "Then I shall have to give the lady what she wants."

The sound of her voice, being naughty and yet so shy, did something to him. The tangle of need inside of him was too intense. He got up, adjusting her lying down on the chaise lounge. Then he positioned himself on top of her, gently and reverently. The thought that someone might barge in on them and catch them in the act only seemed to heighten his desire for her because her body was so ready for him, for the sensation of feeling him deep inside of her.

He lowered himself and kissed her neck, and that sent a million little goosebumps down his back. He could feel the tip of his manhood stretching her again, that burning heat that felt so good. Her fingers rested on his shoulders as her legs locked around him, refusing to let go.

The slide of his manhood inside of her was effortless and pleasurable. He stole her breath as he lodged deep inside of her, only to start moving in and out slowly. He kissed her throat again, traveling up to her earlobe. She moaned loudly, her breath hot against his skin.

Then he started thrusting deeper and deeper, and she clutched on to him as if holding for her dear life. Her body trembled beneath him as his movements became more rushed, more needful. Her restraint weakened completely, and she let go. He watched her as pleasure unfurled from deep inside of her while she still gripped onto him, refusing to let go.

A moment later, his own body followed suit. He stiffened inside of her, spilling his seed into her as their foreheads touched. He never wanted to leave the warmth of her being, the sensations that enveloped them both. A moment later, he slumped next to her, both of them mindless with pleasure.

Still breathing heavily, she turned to him. "So what was that declaration, my lord?"

He smiled, inhaling deeply. "That I love you," he murmured. "That I will never ask you to be anything but *exactly* who you are, that I want this life with you, as you are."

Catharine's eyes shimmered at him, wide and clear. And when she kissed him again, it was slow and certain, completely unshaken by any doubts.

Was it unorthodox? Yes.

But also unmistakably theirs.

Chapter Twenty-Eight

"...and then Margaret started weeping, but truly weeping, because the swan wouldn't eat the bread from her hand." Eliza exploded into a chuckle with her eyes bright over the rims of her teacup.

"I was six!" Margaret cried, scandalised and red-cheeked, nearly spilling her tea as she swatted at Eliza's sleeve. "And I had named him Percival, and he was my friend. You were both horrid."

Catharine smiled over the delicate edge of her porcelain cup, enjoying the scent of lavender and bergamot. "You declared he had chosen you and sobbed into your pinafore when he bit your thumb."

Margaret gasped in mock outrage. "You remember that?"

"I remember everything," Catharine said, soft but teasing. "Including the time you convinced the stable boy to sneak you into the orchard after midnight because you were quite sure a fairy prince had left you a love note."

Eliza choked on her tea.

Margaret covered her face with both hands, groaning. "I was thirteen, and Eliza said it looked like a fairy's handwriting!"

"I said it looked like *someone's* handwriting," Eliza countered, laughing. "I didn't say it wasn't Thomas the gardener's."

All three women dissolved into laughter. It was easy here, in the quiet warmth of the drawing room, far from the eyes and expectations of society. The tea tray sat between them, while the half-finished biscuits and lemon tarts were left ignored in favour of stories.

"It's strange," Margaret said after a moment, settling back against the settee's cushions with one foot curled beneath her, "how everything changes and somehow stays the same. We used to whisper about our futures under the covers like they were fairy tales. And now look at us."

Catharine's smile softened. "Some of it was a fairy tale."

Eliza raised a brow. "Yours or mine?"

"Neither," Catharine murmured, but there was no bitterness about her response, for what they both had was something truer.

"Yes, we grew up," Eliza murmured as she glanced down at her wedding band, twisting it absently on her finger. "We married men with tempers and secrets and pasts, and still... here we are, stronger than we were."

"Speak for yourself," Margaret huffed dramatically. "I haven't married anyone with a secret past or a title, or even a decent sense of punctuality."

"That's because you turn down every suitor you meet," Eliza said with a smirk.

"They're dull," Margaret insisted.

Catharine laughed again, reaching across the table to take her hand. "You'll find someone, dearest. Or maybe he'll find you. Or maybe," she added with a teasing tilt of her head, "you'll climb onto a tree one day, and you won't be able to climb down, and he'll be there."

"Like you," Margaret grinned, eyes sparkling.

"I was thrown from a horse, not lured by a tree," Catharine corrected with mock indignation.

Eliza lifted her brow. "But you did end up tangled in a rather poetic romance all the same. I think that counts."

Margaret reached for a biscuit, hesitated, and then set it down untouched. Catharine's gaze flicked towards her, noticing the shift and the sudden stillness in her youngest sister's movements, in the way her fingers nervously twisted a thread loose on her sleeve.

Eliza caught it too. "Margaret?"

"I..." Margaret looked up, cheeks flushed but not with embarrassment this time. "I think..." She exhaled, then gave a sheepish little smile. "I think I may have someone in mind."

Both Catharine and Eliza sat up straighter at once.

"Oh?" Eliza said carefully, setting her teacup down with exaggerated gentleness, as though not to startle the confession away. "Do go on."

Margaret rolled her eyes but couldn't quite hide her grin. "I knew the moment I said it you'd both pounce."

"I am *sitting,* thank you," Catharine said dryly, though her heart was already beginning to beat a little faster. Margaret so rarely kept anything secret, and when she did, it meant something.

"Who is he?" Eliza asked. "Anyone we know?"

"He was only just introduced into society last month," Margaret said, smoothing the front of her gown as though it helped organise her thoughts. "He's not titled. Not wealthy either, not really. His father's a country doctor... I think he's the younger son of a cousin or something, but he's educated, kind, witty in that way that sneaks up on you rather than shouting for attention."

Catharine leaned forward, resting her chin lightly on her hand. "And he *sees* you?"

Margaret's eyes darted to hers and held.

"Yes," she said quietly. "He listens when I speak. He really listens. He doesn't just try to impress me or flatter me."

Eliza laughed softly. "A rare specimen indeed."

Eliza gasped. "The one who quoted Byron at Lady Holloway's musicale?"

"I thought he was quoting Cicero," Catharine murmured.

Margaret nodded, her face pink. "He was quoting both."

That drew a laugh from all of them, but it softened quickly in tenderness and love.

"You really like him," Catharine said, not as a question.

Margaret was quiet for a moment, and then she nodded. "I do. I don't know where it will lead. But when he looks at me, I don't feel silly or young or like someone waiting to become someone else. I just... feel like me."

The words struck something deep and familiar in Catharine, and judging by the sudden stillness across Eliza's face, in her, too. They sat in silence for a long moment, the kind that only ever passed between people who truly knew one another.

"I hope he's worthy of you," Eliza said at last, like a conclusion.

"If he's not," Catharine added with a faint, wicked smile, "we'll simply have to destroy him."

Margaret snorted. "How comforting."

Catharine reached for her hand again, lacing their fingers. "You deserve a man who will meet you where you are, not one who asks you to shrink. Remember that."

Margaret looked between them, her eyes suddenly too bright.

"I learned that from watching you both," she revealed. "From seeing how you love, and how you're loved in return."

That silenced them.

Then Eliza, who was usually the first to break through emotion with grace, let out a small sniff. "Well, that's quite enough sincerity for one afternoon. Someone pour more tea before I start crying into the scones."

Margaret laughed, wiping at her eyes. "You always cry at the scones."

Catharine smiled as she reached for the teapot, the light catching on her ring as she poured. They were women now, full of bruises and bright dreams, more certain in themselves than they'd ever been as girls.

And still, somehow, they were still each other's safe harbour.

***

That evening, Catharine stepped inside the dining hall, and for a heartbeat, she couldn't speak. The soft flicker of flame reflected off crystal, off polished silver and gilded china, turning the room into something that shimmered gently like memory, or even a dream.

And there they all were.

Margaret waved excitedly from her seat, elbowing Isadora beside her, who offered a sly grin and a wink. Eliza sat opposite them with Rhys, who, by the amused lift of his brow, had said something dry enough to earn Eliza's quiet smirk. Even Dorian was there, reclining a little too comfortably beside Alaric, who stood at the head of the table in a midnight-black coat, looking at her as if she were the only light in the room.

She blinked, overwhelmed. Then she smiled.

"What... what is all this?" she asked, though the answer was already in the details.

The table was dressed in soft ivory and gold, with elegant arrangements of sweet peas and violets, which had been her favourite since girlhood. The scent drifted towards her in delicate waves. The first course had already been served: leek and potato soup with thyme, followed by a dish she instantly recognised: roast pheasant with white wine and tarragon cream, and the spiced carrots done just so. Everything was familiar. Everything was perfect.

Alaric stepped towards her, offering his hand as if it were a dance. "Happy birthday, my love."

"You did all this?" she whispered.

He dipped his head slightly, the corners of his mouth curved in that crooked, almost boyish smile he reserved for her. "I had help, but yes."

She took his hand and leaned up to kiss his cheek, just below the scar. "It's beautiful."

"Not as beautiful as you look right now," he murmured.

Behind them, Margaret groaned audibly. "You two... always ruining my appetite."

"Someone is simply jealous," Eliza teased, folding her napkin with dainty precision.

"Of course I am," Margaret huffed. "Look at this room. If I'm not married by the time I turn twenty-one, I fully expect the same treatment."

Isadora chimed in with a theatrical sigh. "Darling, at twenty-one, I was climbing out of windows to escape dinner parties, not planning them. You'll survive."

Dorian raised his glass. "To climbing out of windows, then."

"To Catharine," Alaric added. He looked only at her as he lifted his glass. "To the woman who makes every room brighter, every life better, and who will never ever stop surprising me."

The others echoed the toast, while laughter and clinks of crystal filled the space around them. Slowly, as they began eating, stories started to unfurl.

Her father was, as ever, attempting to feign gruff disinterest while grumbling about Margaret's mounting list of suitors. "I don't care how poetic this one is," he muttered, pointing a fork. "A man who owns that many cravats cannot be trusted."

Margaret rolled her eyes, but she was glowing with the kind of happiness Catharine remembered from younger days, when belief in romance had not yet been touched by disappointment. "He writes actual verse, Papa. And unlike some people, he doesn't fall asleep during recitations."

"He's likely napping through his own," her father countered, causing the whole table to erupt in a burst of laughter.

On the other end, Rhys and Dorian were locked in a debate over tax reforms, while Isadora leaned back in her chair, swirling her wine with an amused little smirk.

"I'm just saying," she interrupted with feigned sweetness, "any man who writes more letters to his accountant than his wife deserves to be taxed twice."

Catharine laughed behind her hand, her eyes finding Alaric's across the table. He smiled slightly with that quiet smile of his, the one that rarely showed teeth but warmed everything behind his eyes. And then his fingers found hers under the table again, lacing through them without fanfare.

The evening slowly blurred into soft farewells, and laughter pressed into hugs. Coats were fetched, and final glasses of port were offered and politely declined. Margaret yawned dramatically and declared herself too emotionally fulfilled to stay awake another moment. Eliza and Rhys were the last to leave, Eliza catching Catharine's hand with a gentle squeeze and a knowing look that needed no words.

And then it was just the two of them again.

Catharine stood near the hearth of the chamber they now shared, still a little breathless with happiness, when Alaric appeared before her, holding something wrapped in deep blue cloth.

"I have one more thing for you," he offered.

She turned to him, smiling. "You already gave me everything I could've asked for."

She made him smile. "Open it anyway… for me."

The cloth fell away under her fingers, and when she saw what rested within, she stopped breathing. It was a book. Actually, it was a worn, leather-bound volume, with the gold embossing on the spine just beginning to fade.

Her hands trembled as she lifted it, reverent and slow, her thumb brushing over the familiar title: *The Travels of Oriana Vale.*

She hadn't seen this book since she was a child, since it had been left behind one summer, forgotten on a bench in the garden of a house they'd never returned to. She had cried for days, not because it was valuable, but because it had felt like truly hers, like the magic had been written solely for her.

"I..." Her throat tightened as she opened the cover, realizing it was the first edition. "How did you find this?"

"I asked your sisters," Alaric said softly. "It took... longer than I thought it would, but it's finally here, in your hands, where it belongs."

Catharine pressed her fingers to her lips, feeling the tears welling fast and warm. "I... I don't know what to say."

"I wanted you to have it again," he said simply. "I thought... something loved that deeply should be returned."

She couldn't speak. She could barely see through the blur of emotion tightening her chest.

"But to love *you*," he said, his voice a little hoarse, "is the most precious thing in the world."

Without thinking, she threw her arms around him, with the book still clutched between them, and buried her face in his chest. He held her tightly, silently, as though anchoring her there for as long as she needed.

And for a long while, they simply stood like that, wrapped in firelight and memory, in a gift returned and a heart given freely.

Chapter Twenty-Nine

The air held the first whisper of golden autumn, edged with the scent of ripened apples and turned earth. Leaves were just beginning to blush at their tips, and the sky, soft and high above them, was streaked with the pale blue of a season in quiet transition.

The Ravensedge Estate was alive.

There were picnic blankets stretched across the south lawn in a cheerful patchwork: striped linen, fine wool, even one old tartan Catharine remembered draping over their knees in childhood winters. Baskets lay open, brimming with sugared plums, shortbread, wedges of soft cheese, and little pies dusted with nutmeg. Crystal decanters of wine and cordial gleamed in the sun, surrounded by half-empty glasses.

Laughter drifted like music.

Catharine sat under the shade of a great old elm with the hem of her dove-grey gown spread neatly across her lap, though her slippered toes curled into the grass beneath. A breeze teased at the ribbons of her bonnet, and beside her, Margaret lay stretched across a blanket. Her face had that lovely flush from too much sun and too many honeyed pears.

Eliza was just beyond them, seated upright with the quiet poise of a new mother. In her arms, her son wriggled contentedly, a miniature bundle of dark curls and round, serious eyes.

"Oh, he has Rhys' scowl," Isadora declared, crouching beside them and peering down at the baby as if appraising a priceless painting. "That's the face of a future prime minister or possibly a very judgmental poet."

Catharine laughed, reaching to brush a speck of lint from the infant's fine cap. "You poor darling, being burdened with ambition before you can even speak."

"I think he's perfect," Margaret said, sitting up and leaning closer. "His fingers are so tiny."

"He has your mouth," Catharine said to Eliza, smiling.

Eliza looked down, her hand gently cradling the baby's head. "Do you think so?"

"Exactly so," Catharine said with a faintly triumphant expression. "And you should count yourself fortunate. No one wants a baby with your husband's jaw. He probably looked like a grim little soldier from the cradle."

"I heard that," Rhys called lazily from across the lawn, where he stood with Alaric and Dorian near a table laden with bottles and plates. His voice was dry as ever, but the tilt of his mouth betrayed a smile.

The baby gave a soft hiccup, then yawned with a mouth open wide in that astonishing, utterly trusting way only infants could ever manage. Catharine's heart was full of joy.

She didn't know what it was, exactly. Perhaps it was the golden light flickering through the trees, the sound of her sisters' laughter, or the warmth of a baby's cheek pressed briefly against her hand, but something about it felt suspended in amber. It was one of those perfect, ordinary days that passed unnoticed until it was memory.

She leaned back on her hands, tipping her head towards the sky. Birds flitted overhead. Somewhere in the hedges, bees hummed.

Margaret reached for another tart and sighed happily. "If every day were like this, I'd never marry. I'd just stay here forever, fat on pastry and surrounded by babies that aren't mine."

"Then marry someone with a cook," Isadora quipped. "And an aversion to children."

Eliza gave a gentle snort. "You should write a book on matchmaking, Izza. I'm sure it would be *very* well-received."

"I'm full of wisdom," Isadora said, reclining beside them like a satisfied cat, and all of them burst into a chuckle.

That was when Dorian strolled into view, looking every inch the picture of relaxed serenity. There was even a sprig of something green tucked carelessly into his lapel.

"Well, what have I missed?" he called, brushing a leaf from his shoulder. "A scandal? A duel? A family debate over the merits of quince jelly?"

Isadora didn't miss a beat. "You've missed my brilliant insights on infant diplomacy and Margaret's vow to become a pastry-bound spinster."

"Tragic," Dorian said, stepping around the picnic baskets with ease. "I shall carry the grief with dignity."

"You shall carry it with your mouth full," Isadora replied, tossing him a small apple tart. He caught it one-handed, grinning as he sat down far too close beside her.

Catharine raised a brow, watching as Isadora didn't bother shifting away, and strangely enough, neither did he.

"You know, I was late because I was detained by Lady Harcourt," he explained, breaking the tart neatly in half. "She insisted on recounting, in agonizing detail, the unfortunate affair of her neighbour's canary."

"Ah, yes," Isadora sighed dramatically, "the great Avian Tragedy of Belgrave Square. History will never forget."

Dorian handed her the larger half of the tart without looking, and Isadora accepted it with the faintest brush of her fingers against his. Margaret bit her lip to suppress a grin. Eliza exchanged a glance with Catharine, one that was full of amused satisfaction.

"Well," Rhys called from the table, having evidently been listening from across the lawn, "I suppose there's no use pretending anymore."

"I *told* you they were attached," Margaret whispered loudly, elbowing Catharine.

Catharine only smiled, her gaze never leaving the two now pretending not to notice the eyes upon them.

"Attached?" Dorian echoed with faux innocence. "That's a rather broad word. We happen to enjoy each other's company... occasionally... under duress."

Isadora smirked. "Speak for yourself. I merely tolerate him, for the sake of the scenery."

"And the wine," he added.

"Mostly the wine," she agreed with a sweet grin.

Their banter was sharp and fond at the same time, threaded with that unmistakable intimacy born not just of flirtation but of trust. They knew each other. Not only that, but they also *chose* each other. And even in jest, that truth nestled beneath every word.

"Congratulations, although we've known it for a while now," Eliza said warmly, lifting her teacup.

"I had money riding on it," Rhys muttered.

"Rhys." Eliza nudged him with her free elbow, but that only made him lean closer to her and rest a gentle kiss on her forehead.

Dorian, looking not at all chastened, raised his glass to the group. "Well then. To scandal narrowly avoided and to Isadora's very patient heart."

Isadora rolled her eyes, but her smile was unmistakably genuine. "And to your good sense in finally realising you were hopelessly in love with me."

Laughter rippled across the lawn, and upon it, the group settled deeper into their blankets and cushions. Wine was poured again, this time slower, and the golden light had begun to dip towards amber, softening the edges of the world.

Margaret stretched her legs across a patch of grass. "I still can't believe everything's so... calm now, after all that."

Eliza glanced down at the baby asleep against her shoulder. "Calm is earned."

There was a silence then, and it was Rhys who broke it, setting down his glass and brushing a crumb from his cuff.

"Blackmoor has been moved to Newgate," he told them, "under guard. Charges are being finalised, consisting of fraud, bribery, abuse of office... possibly attempted murder, though that will depend on how the witness testimonies hold."

Margaret's eyes widened. "Attempted... He really meant to kill Alaric?"

Alaric's hand, warm and steady, closed gently over Catharine's, where it rested on her knee.

Rhys nodded, his voice level. "The stablehand's account, combined with what Blackmoor attempted at the Lords, is damning enough. He won't walk away from this."

Catharine felt the weight of memory press briefly against her chest. Her entire body recounted the sudden lurch of the horse beneath her, the jarring pain, the sound of Alaric's voice calling her name in the moments after. Her fingers curled slightly into Alaric's palm.

"I still don't understand why he did it," Margaret said quietly. "Why go to such lengths?"

Isadora leaned back, arms folded. "Because power and pride are cruel things when threatened. He thought he was untouchable. Men like that usually do."

"There will be a fallout," Rhys pointed out wisely. "Blackmoor wasn't without allies. Some are scrambling to distance themselves. Others are pretending they were never aligned at all."

"Cowards," Eliza murmured.

"Politicians," Isadora corrected.

Dorian, who had gone unusually quiet, said, "He didn't just want to harm Catharine. He wanted to destroy Alaric, publicly, to make an example of them both."

"He failed," Alaric murmured, more to himself than to anyone else.

Catharine turned her gaze towards her husband. He didn't seem anxious or apprehensive, but the silver in his eyes had a steely edge.

"He failed," she echoed softly.

The wind stirred, rustling through the trees like a secret being carried away.

Rhys refilled his glass, then looked at Catharine with the faintest smile. "The Council's mood has shifted. You've more allies now than you did a month ago. Some of the very ones who tried to shut you out are now citing you as an example of reform."

Catharine raised a brow. "They've a short memory."

"No," Rhys corrected, "they're just opportunists. But for once, their opportunism is working in the right direction."

The tension eased slightly, and Margaret, ever eager to restore cheer, proclaimed, "Well, if we're listing triumphs, I'd like to propose we name this lawn *Victory Hill*. We can plant a tree or perhaps erect a statue."

Dorian looked thoughtful. "Only if the statue is of Isadora in her triumphal bonnet. I mean, just look at all those feathers."

Isadora gave him a flat look. "You're lucky I'm already fond of you, Gainsworth."

Laughter rose again, but Catharine's heart remained still for a moment longer, as Blackmoor's name slowly lifted like fog touched by sunlight. The family had always had a way of righting itself, of tilting back towards joy, no matter how heavy the storm.

"Then perhaps we should name the statue after me," Margaret declared, swiping a ripe blackberry from the nearest dish.

"It would need to be entirely edible," Isadora said loftily, "to match your priorities."

"I would make a *delightful* statue," Margaret replied, waving another blackberry at Isadora. "Artistic and delicious."

"You'd melt in the first heatwave," Eliza teased, cradling her son now peacefully dozing in her arms. "But you'd go out sweetly."

"I'll toast to that," Dorian added, lifting his glass in mock solemnity. "To Miss Margaret of Victory Hill, devoured by children and bees alike."

The group dissolved into chuckles. Even Catharine, who had not said much in the last few minutes, found herself grinning as she tucked a windswept curl behind her ear. As the sun dipped lower and the shadows stretched long across the lawn, Alaric leaned closer.

"Come," he murmured against her temple. "Walk with me."

She didn't need to answer. She only slipped her hand into his, rising from the blanket. They wandered away from the bustle, beyond the trimmed hedgerows and gravel paths, into the quieter edge of the orchard where the air smelled faintly of ripening pears and drying leaves. She thought this was the perfect moment.

"Alaric," she said finally, pausing beneath an arched bough.

He turned towards her at once, his brows lifted slightly.

"I... "—she chuckled a little nervously—"I've been trying to find the right time."

Hc stilled, and his expression was utterly alert now. But he still didn't speak.

"I'm expecting."

His eyes widened, as though the breath had left him entirely, and in the next second, he'd swept her into his arms, lifting her clean off the ground with a low, stunned laugh.

"Catharine," he whispered into her shoulder, "my goodness..."

She was laughing too now, breathless as he spun her once and set her gently down. His hands stayed at her waist and were trembling just slightly.

"You're sure?" he asked, voice barely above a breath. "You're—"

"I'm sure."

He stared at her as though he might never look away again. Then a grin broke across his face, wide and boyish and unguarded.

"I..." He kissed her. "I love you." Another kiss. "I love you, I love you, I—"

She pressed her fingers to his lips, laughing through her own tears. "I know. I know."

He leaned his forehead against hers, still catching his breath. "You've just given me the entire world."

"No," she said softly. "We made it... together."

And there, under the rustling leaves and fading gold of early autumn, Catharine Vale closed her eyes and leaned into the warmth of the man she loved, wrapped in a secret that would become their future.

Epilogue

Years had softened the edges of the world.

The estate no longer echoed with the tremors of scandal or the whispers of doubters. Instead, it pulsed with the slow, steady rhythm of peace, which was hard-won and joy that was now fiercely protected. Even the trees seemed wiser now, arching overhead as Alaric walked the woodland path beside his wife, their hands brushing with every step.

Catharine moved more slowly these days, with the curve of her belly prominent beneath the folds of her walking dress. Her hands often rested instinctively atop it, protective and gentle even in idle thought.

"You know," she pointed out amusedly, "if she climbs that tree again, I'm naming this child Chaos, and that's it."

Alaric followed her gaze to the meadow ahead. Their youngest was halfway up an old willow, with her boots discarded somewhere in the grass and her skirt muddied with stubborn independence. She was a force of nature, that one. All Catharine's defiant fire and his own relentless will, packaged in a laugh that could break kingdoms and stitched together with dimples and mischief.

"She gets that from you, you know," Catharine murmured with an exasperated sigh.

He chuckled. "I beg to differ. You're the one who told her bedtime stories about women who outwitted dragons."

"I told her stories about diplomacy and intelligence triumphing over brute force," she spouted, though with amusement.

He smiled. "You told her how to win."

"And you taught her how not to yield," she added, glancing at him sidelong. "Even when she absolutely should."

Alaric exhaled, the air fresh with the faint perfume of late wildflowers and woodsmoke. The sun cut through the trees in long golden spears, lighting the edges of her hair. Time had changed them both. He was now slightly more silver at his temples, and there was a gentler line at her mouth when she smiled, but it had not worn them down. If anything, it had made them sharper where it mattered and softer where it counted.

They stopped by the edge of the clearing as their daughter launched herself from a low branch, landing with all the grace of a warrior queen.

"Mama! Papa! Did you see?"

Alaric cupped his hands to his mouth. "I saw *someone* fly straight out of a tree without permission."

The little girl beamed, utterly unrepentant. "I landed perfectly!"

Catharine's hand tightened on his arm. "She's going to give me grey hair."

"She already has," Alaric teased her. Then he leaned closer as his lips brushed her temple. "But they look good on you."

She laughed, resting her head briefly against his shoulder.

The child tore back towards them with her feet pounding and her arms outstretched. As she reached them, Alaric caught her easily beneath the arms and lifted her high into the air, spinning her once before settling her between them.

"You're muddy," he told her with mock severity.

"I'm *brave*," she countered, beaming between them.

Catharine smoothed her daughter's wind-tangled hair, one hand still cradling her belly. "You can be both, darling. But brave girls still take baths."

The child made a face. "I suppose."

A sudden rustle came from behind the nearest weeping willow tree. Alaric turned around, already tensing, for old instincts in him had never quite died. But before he could say a single word, a small figure leapt out with a triumphant squeal.

"Boo!"

Catharine jolted just slightly before bringing a hand to her chest in mock alarm. Alaric clutched his heart theatrically, staggering back a step.

"Saints preserve us!" he gasped. "We're under attack!"

From behind the curtain of long willow leaves emerged their middle daughter, Lily. Her brown curls were bouncing as she ran, and her cheeks were flushed with mischief.

"I got you!" she declared, planting her fists on her hips with all the grandeur of a conquering general.

"You did indeed," Catharine said, recovering with a smile that didn't quite hide her affection. "You're growing stealthier by the day."

"I practiced for hours," Lily said proudly, then shrieked as a blur of motion came charging through the grass behind her.

Her sister Rose, still barefoot and wild from her butterfly chase, collided into her with the force of a well-aimed cannonball. The two girls collapsed into a giggling heap, tangled in each other's arms and laughter.

"Careful," Alaric called over to them, trying not to smile. "You'll scare away all the woodland spirits."

"We *are* the spirits!" Lily shouted back, throwing her arms up.

Catharine laughed under her breath, shaking her head as the girls took off across the meadow again with their hands clasped together. Then she exhaled next to him, her hand instinctively brushing the curve of her bourgeoning belly again.

"I hope this one will be a calm boy," she murmured. "I deserve a calm boy. A thoughtful one... quiet. Preferably one who naps."

Alaric chuckled, arching a brow as he turned to her. "You mean one like me?"

She gave him a dry look. "You have never been calm a day in your life."

"I'm calm now," he pointed out, mockingly wounded.

"You're leaning against a tree like a smitten poet and trying to look down my dress every time I breathe."

"I call that focus, not chaos."

She laughed despite herself, nudging him with her shoulder. "If this child comes out with your mischief and my stubbornness, we'll have to move to the countryside just to contain him."

"We already live in the countryside," Alaric said, gesturing around them.

"Further," she replied, deadpan. "Scotland, perhaps. An island."

Alaric tilted his head, as if considering. "That actually wouldn't be so bad. I've always wanted a castle surrounded by goats and gale winds. I could wear tartan. You could teach our wildling children how to duel in French."

She sighed dramatically, but her smile was radiant. "You're impossible."

"And you love me."

"I do."

He turned to her fully then, his hand resting over hers where it lay on her belly.

"Whatever this one is, boy, girl, calm or not, they'll have the best of you. And hopefully," he added with a wink, "a bit of my charm."

"God help us," she murmured, rolling her eyes playfully at him.

"Indeed," Alaric added in mock solemnity.

The afternoon stretched into pleasant oblivion until that evening, when Alaric stepped inside the drawing room with two cups of tea. His wife sat curled on the chaise, wrapped in a thick shawl with her hair loose around her shoulders and her expression drowsy. Her book lay forgotten at her side.

He handed her one of the cups, letting their fingers brush as she looked up at him with a quiet smile.

"All settled upstairs?" she asked softly.

Alaric sank down beside her, the cushions giving beneath his weight.

"If by *settled* you mean Izza thrilling the girls with a thoroughly inaccurate tale of pirates and wolves to stall bedtime, then yes."

Catharine chuckled lightly. "We'll have to thank her for making bedtime last an hour longer."

He slipped his arm behind her shoulders, drawing her close. "Not now," he murmured. "Now you're warm and quiet. And no one is crawling on you or asking for more jam."

She gave a small, amused sigh and leaned into him, resting her head on his chest. He breathed her in, that scent he knew so well: faint lavender, paper, and the familiar trace of her skin warmed by firelight.

A thought materialised in his mind.

His daughters. His wife. His *home.*

The peace that stretched around them wasn't loud or showy. It wasn't the thunder of victory or the sharp taste of triumph. It was quiet—the kind of quiet a man bled for, the kind that felt sacred.

He felt Catharine shift slightly against him and looked down at the curve of her belly.

"Do you remember," she said, her voice little more than a whisper, "how I used to think none of this was possible?"

Alaric didn't answer right away. Instead, he reached for her hand and lifted it to his lips, pressing a kiss to her knuckles. "I remember," he said. "And I remember how you made it happen anyway."

She tilted her head up and smiled at him. "*We* made it happen."

He brushed a loose curl behind her ear. "You started it. You walked into my study with blood in your voice and fire in your eyes. You made me see the world differently."

She leaned up and kissed him.

"You loved me when I didn't know how to be loved," she murmured against his mouth.

"And you loved me when I didn't think I deserved to be."

Their foreheads touched. For a while, they just breathed. Alaric looked around the room, listening to the faint tick of the longcase clock marking time.

Years ago, he'd thought he'd lost everything that mattered. Now he couldn't imagine what more he could ask for.

"I think," he whispered tenderly, "this is what happiness is."

Catharine's fingers threaded through his. "Yes," she whispered back. "I think so too."

And as the fire crackled low and the house settled for the night, Alaric Vale, the Marquess of Ravensedge, held the woman he adored and the quiet world they'd built together, finally and truly at peace.

THE END

Also by Valentina Lovelace

Thank you for reading "**A Wicked Match for the Marquess**"!

I hope you enjoyed every moment! If you did, you're welcome to explore **my full Amazon Book Catalogue here:**

https://go.valentinalovelace.com/bc-authorpage

Thank you for helping me bring my dream to life! ❤

Printed in Dunstable, United Kingdom